The Dating Experiment

The Dating Experiment

The Dating Experiment

Kelli Rajala

2021

The Dating Experiment

First Printing: 2021

ISBN 978-0-578-83403-0

www.facebook.com/Kerajala41

Kelli Rajala

Too all of my friends, family, teachers, and
anyone else who has ever supported my writing endeavors.

Thank you!

CONTENTS

The Dating Experiment

T'WAS THE NIGHT BEFORE IT BEGAN

THE FIRST MAN I had dated in six years was a sheep (not a real one, don't worry), all thanks to my older sister, Ava, the serial dater. She was the type to bring home a (decidedly new version) of the same guy every other week. And, unimpressed with my lack of dating combined with her interest in finding a whole *new* type of guy, (one who might last, perhaps), she signed us both up for a blind dating game.

At thirty-one years old, Ava wanted to settle down. She wanted kids. She wanted steady. More than anything, she wanted stable. For her twenty-six-year-old "baby" sister, she wanted a lost virginity and less reason to bitch and moan every Valentine's Day. Admittedly, I couldn't argue with her on those two accounts. I did, however, initially object to the dating game itself, or experiment, as the company liked to call it.

"You do realize this means we're going to have to walk around the city in animal heads looking like a bunch of high school mascots, right?" I'd asked, just to make sure she fully understood what she was getting us both into.

It was the night before the big day. Cinnabun, my rather large French Lop, was snuggling in my lap as I watched Ava rifle through my closet from the safety of my bed. Apparently, I wasn't to be trusted picking out my own date outfit. At least, not for the initial meeting. First impressions and all that. (Insert eye roll.)

"It'll be fun. It's not like it's just going to be you and me. Everyone else will have one too. And there's like... twenty-eight people per month, I believe."

"I'll try to remember how fun it is when I realize that I've come home with a serial killer after what would have been a noticeably sketchy appearance to the naked eye was conveniently hidden behind that of a cute puppy face."

"Ha. Ha. Please, just try this out for me, will you? I'm planning on taking it very seriously."

"I already said I'd do it."

"Good. Then stop whining about it."

She pulled a simple summer dress out of my closet and threw it at me. It was one of my more favorites, a pale, floral, chiffon dress that went to my knees and buttoned at the top.

"I'm surprised you picked this one," I admitted. "It's so modest."

"Yes, but it's also cute, feminine, and perfectly 'you.'

Anything else wouldn't have the right first impression. Plus, you have those really cute pink peep-toe heels that will look *killer* with it."

"And here I was, afraid that you would pick something that better suited *your* tastes."

She laughed and shook her head.

"I want the men I'm matching with to be keeping their eyes on me, not my little sister."

"Good point."

"Besides, if we're going to find you a man, we're going to have to find one who likes you for who you are, not because the first thing he sees is a nice piece of ass."

"Please don't use those words to describe me ever again."

She shook her head and retreated to her own room. (Finally.)

I hadn't been living with my sister for very long. Only a year prior had I graduated from college after changing my major three times. Once that part of my life was over, I was left relatively broke and with the whole world in front of me. Unfortunately, I didn't know what to do with myself, so instead of venturing out on my own, I moved in with my sister in the city.

Things were working out just fine between us, but we

definitely had our differences. It had otherwise been so long since we had lived together, that I had seemingly forgotten how crazy she could be. It was a good kind of crazy, if I was being honest with myself. I just needed to adjust to it, and for some reason a year simply hadn't been an ample amount of time for me to do so yet.

"Well, Cinnabun, here's to hoping for the best of luck." She wiggled her nose at me, which I took as a sign that she had, in fact, wished me luck. "I think it's time to go to bed, though. It's getting pretty late."

I got up and set Cinnabun back in her cage for the night, then checked to make sure that her food and water were all good. She snuggled into her little blanket in the back as always and, when I was done, I got ready for bed, myself.

One of the reasons I hadn't dated in so long was because I simply wasn't good at it. I'd always been quiet and awkward, and I almost never noticed if a guy so much as looked at me twice. Dating was for social people, not bookworms who sipped wine in fuzzy socks on both Friday and Saturday nights, because they genuinely believed that was more fun than "going out."

I sucked at small talk. I was literally one of those "So how's the weather?" girls. I responded to most things, unintentionally, with one-word answers. Oh. Cool. Nice.

Awesome. Okay. Wow. Neat. I never knew what to say. I felt bad for the poor suckers that were going to get matched with me. Maybe I'd get lucky and they'd all be chatty types, the kind that you wish would just shut up already, except when you're a girl like me, who relishes in other people taking over the conversation for her, because she otherwise couldn't handle it. Yes. There was hope.

My thoughts went on like this all night, so even after brushing my teeth, putting on my pajamas, and snuggling down into the burrito of warmth and comfort that was my two thick blankets, I still could not fall asleep. I simultaneously loved and hated Ava for getting me into this.

Steady, my beating heart. This is isn't a marriage proposal I'm walking into tomorrow, I reminded myself. *If this doesn't go well, then I'm done. I don't have to go through with the whole thing. If I fail to meet a guy, I fail to meet a guy. No big deal. I can go back to staring at them from afar, and living vicariously through Ava.*

THE EXPERIMENT

"ELLA!"

We didn't have to be at the Hall until 10:00 a.m. It was currently only 6:00 a.m. At first, I couldn't even begin to imagine why Ava was waking me up at this ungodly hour when she knew that I didn't have a lot of getting ready to do, and then it hit me...

"Oh... right. I couldn't sleep," I called back.

Ava came storming into my bedroom from the bathroom, looking like she wanted to wring my neck.

"So you organized my entire makeup supply? I thought we agreed that your obsessive need to organize would be limited to *your* things only."

"And public spaces," I added.

"The bathroom isn't a public space."

"True, but did I mention not being able to sleep? I needed something to do, and the bathroom was a mess. Now it's not. You're welcome."

"I had a system!"

"Yes, and now you have an *organized* system. You'll find everything just fine. I included labels."

She gave me one last stern look before stomping her way back to the bathroom. I rolled over to try and catch a few more hours of sleep.

Good morning to you too, Ava.

-

A few years ago, when the Dating Experiment started to become popular enough to reel in a decent amount of cash, the original developers custom designed a building to hold introductions, the formal ball, and any other meeting of the whole group of participants. Because of this, the building was split in two, each half mirroring the other. We were told to park in lot B on the East side and enter through the East door. Once we did so, slightly after the hour (Ava's fault), we were met with a line of twelve other women queued up to the registration desk.

"Thanks for making us last," I commented. "It's a good thing the guys won't know. First impressions and all that," I reminded her with a smirk.

Ava only rolled her eyes.

I looked around at the other women, sizing them up, I suppose. It was dumb to judge them based on what they looked like, I knew, but I couldn't help looking anyway. It seemed they had all dressed their very best and spent hours on hair and makeup, even though nobody would be able to see all of the effort they put in besides us other women.

As each one passed through registration they were given their "mask," or rather, the cartoonish head of a random animal. We were told we would have to put them on before being allowed to enter the next room, so most of them didn't hesitate, and the resulting image was... amusing, to say the least. Everyone looked like part of the entertainment for a child's birthday party getting suited up.

"Ava and Ella Carter," my sister announced as we finally approached the table.

She passed our IDs to one of the two women seated there, who then checked us off the list and handed us an itinerary, and a small sheet of paper with three animals listed on it. Mine: Sheep, Koala, Mouse. I supposed those were my dates. There was no other information.

I was given the last head, a joyfully cute panda bear. Ava was given the cheetah. In a way, it was fitting. She was fast, on the go, fierce. I was that panda in the online video that rolls around on the ground until it eventually gets stuck on something, and then has to spend the next five to ten minutes trying to figure

16

out how to get unstuck. I secured it on my head and breathed a sigh of relief. It didn't have that weird-forty-year-old-high-school-mascot scent.

"Alright!" announced lady number one, the blonde who had taken our IDs. "Everyone in a line, quiet down! We're going to make our way into the Center. It will be the room in which we'll always be meeting together with the men, whenever such a situation should be called for. You are to sit in any of the chairs available, but remain quiet, as you are not allowed to fraternize at this point. Here, you will be given your formal introduction."

Some of the women were already giggling as lady number two, a short brunette, finally opened the door. Lady number one shushed them.

I didn't understand their excitement Once we were all ushered into the large room there wasn't much to see. I mean, the room itself was pretty nice, ornately decorated in reds and golds and all that, but the men looked just about the same as us. Random, adorable animal heads on top of regular, human bodies, scattered about the seating. We were basically a bunch of clothed Beanie Babies.

I grabbed a seat in the back row between a cat and a raccoon, while Ava ended up somewhere in the middle. A woman in a black suit approached the podium at the front of our group.

The Dating Experiment

The founder, I supposed. Or one of them, at least.

"Hello, and welcome to the Blind Dating Experiment! As some of you may know, my name is Holly Van Warden, and I am one of the co-founders of the Dating Experiment. We started this company as a small group of individuals who believed modern societies methods of dating were simply too surface level. We live in an age where you get to swipe left or right on a person after only a glance at their photos. Some of you, like us, may fear that this takes away from the possibility of a genuine connection.

"However, some of you may be here for the sole purpose of trying something new and exciting, and that's okay too. Whatever your reason, we admire your sense of vulnerability and courage, because this is no simple dating experience you've all signed yourselves up for.

"In the beginning, we had asked you to fill out a rather thorough questionnaire as part of the application process. Along with our team of specialists, we've compiled a short three-person list for each of you with your top three matches. Your first three dates will be with each respective person on your list, after which you will choose which of your partners you would like to continue dating long-term. Please understand that, though you may put one person first on your assessment list, you may not be first on theirs. It will be up to our specialist to sort out top couples.

Remember you are also allowed to make changes after this point. Your choice is not set in stone."

(And that is how my first date in six years was a sheep).

"The rules from here on out are pretty simple," Holly continued. "Once we come to long-term dating, each partner will alternate turns. There are three tasks you must complete on every date. Number one, you have to come up with some sort of gift to give your date, whether that be handmade, or store bought. Number two, you must choose an activity for your date, such as going to a movie, or riding bicycles together. Number three, you must choose your dining experience. This can be in the form of a sit-down restaurant, or even fast food if that is what you wish.

"The twist involved with these tasks we've set for you is this: Your partner gets to be honest with you about whether or not they liked your choices. For each choice you get right, you are permitted one question about anything you wish relating to your partner's life, and/or who they are as a person. You are not, however, to ask questions about their appearance, as that eliminates the purpose of your masks.

"During your dates, you are not allowed to take off said masks, nor are you to take the information you've learned about a person to do research on the side. Well we assure you there will be no spying or monitoring of your behavior on our end, we'd like to remind you that you most likely did not pay the fifty dollar application fee simply to come here and cheat. If you wish to enjoy the full experience of the Blind Dating Experiment, it would be wise to play by the rules.

"Lastly, your itinerary will show you when we will be having group meet-ups to go over anything and everything that may be of concern to you, and when the Reveal Ball will be. This is an important event. Although some of the meetings are listed as optional, the Ball is not. This is where you will finally be able to take your masks off and meet face-to-face for the very first time, hopefully having made a deep and meaningful connection beforehand. It's a very special moment and, in all honesty, a very lovely opportunity to dress up and have a party.

"On that note, are there any questions you'd like to ask regarding the rules I've thus far stated?" She waited, but the herd stayed quiet. "Excellent! This evening will consist of dinner date number one, where you will each head off with the first person on your list. For this round only, it will be the men taking the ladies out each time. Your contact information has already been swapped. We wish you good luck, and that you may find that special someone you've always been waiting for!"

According to the itinerary, our first date was set for anywhere between 5:00-8:00 PM, dater's choice. While the rest of the room filled with murmurs of excitement, I sought out Ava, hoping to get out and get the panda head off quickly. Unfortunately, she was heavily engaged with the skunk next to her. Leave it to my sister to already have made a new friend. I sat down in an empty chair beside them and waited as patiently as I could manage.

TOO "DAY-TIME" FOR A DINNER DATE

"WELL, THAT WAS fun."

"I detect heavy notes of sarcasm," Ava observed.

"What? No. It was a blast! It's not like they could have just sent us all of that information in a pamphlet or something...."

"And the masks?"

"Packages are mail-able too," I pointed out. "No one was stopping them."

"Except maybe their financial adviser."

The elevator ride back up to our fifth-floor apartment was practically its own version of the walk of shame, especially when we stopped at the second floor and another woman got on. She took note of the panda and the cheetah, trying to hide her smug smile. After all, everyone in the Bay City area who wasn't living under a rock knew about the Dating Experiment. Ava, of course, gave her a polite smile. I looked the other way.

Once back in our apartment, I tossed the panda head in the corner of my bedroom and then fell face first into my pillows. (Note that TV shows and movies don't tell you that this is actually a semi-painful action for your poor nose if your pillows aren't literal clouds.)

"I hope these guys are considerate about the fact that we ladies need time to get ready," said Ava. "If we're going by their schedule we could end up getting only five minutes notice."

"Unless they've never met a woman in their lifetime, I don't think that'll be an issue."

"They could do it out of spite."

"Not if they actually take this seriously."

"I'll just pick an outfit that could go with any kind of date."

"You're changing outfits?" I questioned. "Why?"

She rolled her eyes.

"This is too 'day-time' for a dinner date, which is what we'll be going on in case you haven't figured that out."

Oh, I *had* figured that out. I just didn't care enough to change outfits. What I had on was cute. It would do just fine.

After getting up to feed Cinnabun a few small apple slices, I let her out of her cage to roam around the apartment. When I first got her a little less than a year ago, Ava and I had bunny-proofed all the rooms so she couldn't get in or under anywhere too small to hide. Thankfully, she wasn't as shy around us now, but we kept all the precautions just in case. When we were little we had a kitten that we lost for two days. She had crawled into a hole that was ripped into the back of our old couch. No more taking chances.

"*You* love me, though, right Cinnabun?" I asked.

She wiggled her little nose at me and then hopped out of my room.

Well... maybe not so much, then.

I stayed sitting on my floor and leaned back against my bed. A moment later, Ava peeked around the doorframe.

"See, this is why you need a man," she observed.

I rolled my eyes.

Her commentary was perfect timing, however, because before I could come up with some snide remark, my phone dinged. Ava and I both looked at each other for only a second before I sprang up off the floor and she sprang into the room, both aimed at my bed. Thankfully, I got there first, as I had intentionally gotten in her way.

"It's my phone!" I called out as I quickly grabbed it off my pillow.

"Is it your date?" she asked excitedly, grabbing my shoulders and leaning around me to get a better look.

It was, in fact, my date.

[Sheep]: I'm looking forward to our date! I made reservations for dinner. Just take the bus to West Lincoln and I'll meet you there. At 5:45-ish.

"Oh my, God! I can't believe you got your date details before me!" she practically shouted. "You don't even care about getting ready."

I ignored her, as per usual when she made these types of comments.

"I'm glad he picked West Lincoln," I said instead. "That's a busy part of the city. Lots of witnesses."

She face-palmed and then left my room. I was glad, too, because I needed a moment to be alone. I didn't want her to see how nervous and freaked out I actually was. My heart was hammering away, and all over again I was starting to question if this was really something I wanted to be doing. Sadly, I knew this would have been a rude time to back out, though, so I told myself I needed to go through with it anyway.

-

At 5:30 p.m. I left our apartment and made my way to the bus station. Unfortunately, because I never knew where he could be, I had to leave the house with my panda head already secured snuggly over my own. I sighed as I walked up the steps to the station and caught everyone's gaze turning in my direction. There was no sheep in the vicinity. I think it would have eased my nerves if he had been on the same bus route. At least then I wouldn't have been alone.

Just as I was beginning to feel even more pathetic, however, a late arrival ran up to the bus shouting for it not to leave yet. Once she was on and had paid the fare, she looked around the bus, spotting me instantly. A girl with the head of a deer. She rushed back and joined me, even though we had no idea who the other person even was, let alone whether or not we knew each other.

"I am *so* glad you're here," she said. "You have no idea how good it feels to see someone else in one of these damn heads."

She tapped her knuckles on the side of her deer mask.

"Actually, the feeling's pretty mutual," I answered.

She held out a hand.

"My name's Katie."

"Ella."

We shook hands. I had never considered this a way to meet friends. I knew Ava was going to, but I hadn't thought about it for myself. In all honesty, my only real friend in this city *was* Ava. My sister. And she always thought that was just as sad as my lack of boyfriends. I mean, I had a lot of friends in high school, and some in college, but once I graduated I just stopped meeting people for some reason. After all, I had never been particularly good at talking to strangers. In this moment, however, something about having my true identity hidden made the prospect much less scary.

"That's a pretty name," said Katie.

"Thanks. Is Katie short for anything?"

"Katherine."

(Remember now, no one-word answers!)

"Cool... so... how do you feel about this whole Dating Experiment... thing?"

She shrugged.

"I can't tell yet, I guess. Part of me is excited, and part of me is sick to my stomach right now. I've never had a boyfriend before. I feel silly admitting that at twenty-three, but it's true. I just figured this might be a better way for me to meet a genuine guy looking for something real, you know?"

"Yeah. I get that. I haven't dated much either, so I'm kind of in the same boat."

"The best of luck to both of us then!"

The Dating Experiment

My stop came up before Katie's. We said our good-byes. I turned around to wave at her as I got off the bus, and she waved back. I wondered if I would end up running into her again, and kind of hoped that I would.

There were a lot of people walking about, as this was more of the entertainment part of town and people were off to movies and clubs and other fun places. I glanced around and, eventually, my eyes landed on my mystery man in a sheep's head standing in front of some hipster hangout coffee shop. Part of me really wanted coffee, but this wasn't my date to take over.

"Hi," I mumbled as I approached him.

"Hello!" came a much deeper voice than I had been expecting. He wasn't a very big man after all. "May I?"

He held out his arm in a very old-fashioned, gentlemanly way. I hooked mine through his, feeling a tad silly, but deciding to roll with it anyway. We walked away from the coffee shop, heading down the street in the direction that the ground slanted, forming a decent hill all the way down to Emmett Avenue. Even though it wasn't that steep, my feet in heels didn't enjoy the downward slant. I was suddenly thankful for Sheep's arm holding me steady.

And after a sentence like that, I couldn't help but hope that I would soon be able to refer to my mystery man by an actual

Kelli Rajala

name.

JUNGLE BASH

WE ARRIVED IN front of one of those themed clubs that I vaguely remembered Ava having talked about before. I groaned internally, having wished that we would avoid all of the packed, noisy clubs. The theme for this one was Jungle Bash, unsurprisingly. Amidst all the other dancers wearing animal masks, suits, ears, tails, and other parts, we fit right in. (I think they coordinated with the Dating Experiment.) Smart idea on my dates part, if it wasn't for the fact that I couldn't dance and hated trying. (Oh, and large crowds of sweaty people.)

The moment he opened the door, the thumping bass came pounding into my ears. Lights were flashing. The sounds of animal and bird noises could be head over everything else. Bodies looked tightly pressed together and I was pretty sure I could pick up the scents of sweat and alcohol. I followed the Sheep, because that's what I was supposed to do.

Pushing through the crowd was difficult. I almost lost him

several times as we made our way to the bar. He ordered for me. A pink raspberry cosmo. Not bad, but I would have liked to order for myself. He then ordered himself a scotch. I sipped slowly, following him over to a corner with circular, plush couches. He sat down, patting the spot at his side.

When I sat down next to him, he leaned in to shout into my ear... spot.

"I don't know if you've ever been to this place, but it's pretty cool. My buddies and I come here from time to time."

"No. I haven't been."

"No way. Well, come on then, let's dance!"

(Dude. We *just* sat down!)

He stood up anyway, grabbed my hand, and pulled me out onto the dance floor. My drink sloshed out of the glass and onto a few of the people we were now making our way through. No one seemed to notice, or maybe they just didn't care. My bet was the latter.

Most of the "dancing" was more along the lines of grinding and thrusting. We stopped somewhere in the middle of the crowd and then he let me go, turning to face me. I just stood there awkwardly while he began to dance, and took a sip of my now near-empty drink. It seemed to take him a moment to realize that I wasn't dancing.

"You all right?" he yelled into my ear.

"Yeah. I'm fine."

"You not having fun?" he asked.

I shrugged, but tried to smile. Then I remembered he wasn't going to see that, so I turned around and made my way back over to where we had been sitting before. At least we wouldn't have to yell so loud here. Most of the people were on the dance floor.

"What's wrong?"

"Nothing," I answered. "I just... I don't dance."

His shoulders sank.

"Ah. Darn. I picked a bad place to take you for a date then. I'm sorry."

"It's okay."

"Come on."

He stood up and gestured for me to follow him, so I did. When he set down his drink I also set down my own, and together we left the club. Back out on the sidewalk, we kept walking.

"Well, that's one point lost," he noted.

"Uh... yeah. Sorry."

"No need to apologize. It's just the rules of the game. So now that I've failed on picking an activity, would you like to go get something to eat?"

"Sure."

We headed back in the direction we originally came from and he led me inside one of the more hipster-style food places. The name was Bottles & Bites, and was honestly torn between it being clever or just really stupid. Leaning toward the latter. Regardless, I'd heard about it before and, supposedly, it was a good place to go if you wanted something particularly fresh.

We sat at a table in the back and looked over the one-page menu. He ordered zucchini spaghetti and some kind of fruit-infused vitamin water. I decided on a pesto pasta and grilled chicken dish with a cherry ginger fizz for my drink. Then, while we waited for the food after our waiter took our order, we tried to find things to talk about that didn't call for the asking of personal questions. (I found this particularly hard, not being a good conversationalist as it was.)

"This place I happen to come to a lot," he started. "They have a lot of healthier options, so I don't feel like I'm eating bad even if I'm eating out.'

"I haven't been *here* before either. I guess you could say I don't get out much."

"Oh. Well... I hope you like it."

"Thanks."

Thanks? Was that even an appropriate response?

Probably not. There was a long pause where neither of us seemed to know where to go with the conversation, if you could even call it that. (See? I killed it. Already.) It's probably not necessary for me to say this, but he was the one to finally break that silence.

"Oh! I have to give you your gift."

"Oh! Right."

This was something I could work with. Plus, I was excited to see what a total stranger thought was a good gift for a girl he didn't know a thing about.

Sheep reached into his pocket and pulled out a small, silver box with a pink bow on top. He placed it on the table between us and slid it over to me. Jewelry, no doubt. Not a bad choice... so far. I carefully slid the lid off and set it aside. Inside the box was a beautiful pair of pearl earrings, where the pearl was situated in rose gold petals like the center of a flower. I loved them. There was just one problem.

"These are absolutely adorable," I said. Somehow he picked up on the lingering tone of my voice.

"But..."

I hated to have to say it.

"But... I don't have my ears pierced."

The sheep's cheerful expression was unable to change, and yet somehow he still managed to look dejected. Maybe it was in the way he sat perfectly still, unmoving and quiet, or the way he looked down at the table for a moment, clearly reflecting on our so far short, but still somehow awkward, date.

"I guess I assumed most women these days have their ears pierced. Another point loss for me."

He wasn't wrong, though. I just wasn't "most women."

"If it makes you feel any better," I said, "I may just consider getting them pierced so I can wear these cute earrings. I really do like them."

He perked up a bit.

"That does make me feel a little better," he said. "Do I get half a point for that?"

"Well... I'm not sure how you would ask half a question, but just for the fun of it I'll say yes."

"Man, I hope this food is good."

This time I could hear a smile on his face, so I knew the date wasn't a complete disaster yet. Plus, when the food finally came, it was, in fact, very good. Although challenging to eat through a small mouth slot. That added up to a whole point and a half. I decided that instead of asking something personal, he could ask me something trivial for the half point question.

"Okay," he started. "Personal question first. What are your top three biggest goals in life?"

Hmm... something I hadn't thought about in a while. One of them used to be graduating from college, but I had already done that. Was moving into my own place and starting a family too generic? I mean, anyone could give those answers. Did I even have specific goals that were my own?

"I guess... maybe I'd like to someday have my own business. I love the people I work for now, but... I also have my own style, and I'd like to put it to use."

"Maybe?"

I shrugged.

"I guess. Yeah. I just haven't thought about my goals in a while. I've been so content with everything. But yeah. I'm a sugar artist, so I decorate cookies and things. Sometimes cakes if they're simple. I'd love to do my own designs, not just what my boss draws up for me."

"That's a really cool job, and a great goal."

"Thank you."

See? *Now* it was appropriate.

"Another goal would be to get married. I feel like that's a typical one that doesn't really say much about me as an individual, but that's what it is."

"Still cool. And the third?"

"I don't know... maybe travel to someplace exotic? I've

never been out of the country before, so I think that would be really fun."

"That's one of my top goals too," he said. "I think I've always wanted to go to Japan."

"Japan is on my list as well."

Okay, so this part wasn't going so poorly. In fact, it was sort of relieving to find out we did actually have a few things in common. Maybe he wasn't such a bad choice for me after all, even if we had started out on a bit of a rough foot.

"Alright. Trivial question time. What is your name?"

I smiled a little. I should have known. After all, I was dying to find out his name the whole night. I could see why that was the question he had picked.

"Ella."

"That's a pretty name."

"Thank you!"

"My name's Matthew, but most people call me Matt."

"Nice to meet you, Matt."

Nice to meet you too, Ella."

THE THREE DATES CONTINUED

WHEN I GOT home that night, Ava was dying to hear every detail, so of course I gave them to her.

"Aww! That sounds so cute! That poor guy, though. I'm glad you gave him the half point."

"Me too. So what about your date?" I asked. "How did that go?"

Ava sat down on my bed and grabbed one of my pillows to hold onto while she talked. I held Cinnabun, who had finally ceased roaming the apartment to climb into my lap.

"It was soooo good! First, he gave me my gift, which was this really pretty scented body spray, and I have to say I admire his courage, because that is the kind of gift that is super easy to mess up. Then, he took me on his boat out on the lake and there we had a picnic like dinner of fresh fish and wine. It was honestly the most romantic evening of my life."

Ava spilled the details as though she had been a dam waiting to burst.

"That sounds pretty perfect."

She sighed and wrapped her arms around the pillow to give it a hug.

"I think it was. I liked it all, so I gave him the three points. I hope all of my dates aren't this good, otherwise, I'm going to have a hard time picking which man I want to rate in which order."

I couldn't' help but laugh. My sister *wanted* at least one of her dates to go poorly. Of course, I could see her point. If my next two dates were amazing, I would already know where to put this first one on the list. I just kind of hoped that at least one of them would be as nice as Ava's was for her. I would like the perfect date at least once in my life. (Is that too much to ask for?)

"So he has his own boat?"

"Yes! And oh my God it's so nice."

I let her ramble on about her date for a while longer. Because of this, we stayed up a little later into the night than what I was typically used to. By the end of it all, I was fighting to keep my eyes open and my responses started coming out as mumbled gibberish. It seemed to take her a while to notice this, but when she did, she covered me up with my blanket, shut the light off, and put Cinnabun back in her cage with a small snack and a filled water bottle.

-

The Dating Experiment

I woke up in the morning to my phone buzzing next to my head. Flipping it over to take a look, I saw that I had a new text from an unknown number. I checked, thinking maybe it's Matt and I just hadn't remembered to save his number from last night.

It wasn't.

[Koala]: Good Morning!

Surprised, but still somewhat half asleep, I stared at my phone for a long moment without knowing how to respond. Before I could, I got another one.

[Koala]: I'm thinking lunch, since we all did the whole dinner thing last night already. Sound good?
Me: Sounds good. What time?
[Koala]: 12:00?
Me: Okay.
[Koala]: Great! I'll be at Sam's at noon.

I rolled over and looked at the clock on my bedside table. It was already 11:10 A.M. I needed to get moving! As it was, Sam's Big City Deli was going to be about a ten-minute bus ride from the station nearest our apartment.

I threw on a navy and pink floral dress with a peter pan

collar and short, flow-y sleeves. Then I grabbed my purse, the panda head, and my hot pink heels. I had almost made it out the door by 11:40 when Ava poked her head out of her room.

"Where are you off to already?" she asked.

"Date number two."

"What? So soon?"

What could I say? I had put that I liked to get things done in a timely matter and was a rather punctual person when I filled out the questionnaire. Apparently, they had taken that into consideration. It wasn't my fault they had seemingly given Ava the more leisurely, take-their-time men. I'm just lucky I didn't have to do hair and makeup more than simply throwing my long waves back into a messy bun.

I made it to the station in five minutes by daringly walking without my heels, and climbed on the bus just in time. I would make it to the station nearest Sam's in about seven minutes.

Katie wasn't on the bus this time, nor anyone else from the Dating Experiment, so I sat relatively in the back by myself and sunk down in my seat. Not that there was any way of hiding myself. In all honesty.

The walk to Sam's from the station only took two minutes, so once I was off the bus I arrived right on time. I walked in to find the man with the Koala head already waiting for me at a table. He stood up when he saw me walk through the door.

"Shall we?" he asked, holding out a small menu.

I took it from him and looked it over. His voice was lower than Matt's, and he was taller. So much so, that I was face level with his chest. He was a skinny guy, though, not all broad shoulders and bulky muscles. Of course, that's not what I was supposed to be focusing on, so I picked a sandwich off the menu before it was our turn in line.

We both got turkey club sandwiches with no tomato, his with a Dr. Pepper, mine with a Sprite. We then sat down at the bar in front of the window looking out onto the street. There was a good number of people walking by, as it was a warm Tuesday at the beginning of August. Interestingly, it felt more like summer now that it was almost over. Across the street, I caught a penguin and a frog walking by.

"Hey, look!" I said, pointing at them. "It's another couple."

"Wonder how it's going for them," he added.

"Hopefully less awkward than the date I went on yesterday."

"What? You mean to tell me you've been on a date with another man?"

Confused, I snapped my attention back to him, but there

was no facial expression I could read.

"I... uh..."

I was seriously caught off guard and had no clue how to respond to that, but then he started laughing.

"Okay, no. I'm sorry. That was just a lame joke."
I let myself laugh a little too, though I still felt a bit thrown off.

"It's okay. It was just a tad unexpected."

A server came and brought us our food and drinks. We thanked her as she set everything down. Once she was gone, there was a small moment of silence where we paused the conversation to take our first bites. The food was good, fresh. So far I've ended up with two men that know how to pick a first date meal. Lucky me.

"I'm not going to lie," he said. "I was nervous about doing this... whole thing. You know? I thought it might make me look pathetic."

"Hey now. Watch what you say. I'm here too, after all." He laughed. "But I do know what you mean," I said. "I never would have done this if I wasn't pushed into it by my sister."

This time he nodded.

"It was one of my good friends who decided I needed to put myself out there again," he explained. "It's been several months since I got out of my last relationship, but I've just been...

I don't know, busy maybe? Or unwilling to put the effort in? Maybe that's not what I should be talking about on our first date, though."

I couldn't help but smile.

"It's okay, but what do you mean *first* date? Who's to say we'll pick each other? This could, in fact, be our first *and* last."

He shrugged.

"I guess there *is* no saying. However, unless my third date is spectacular, you don't have much competition."

"Are you saying I couldn't beat the competition if there were any?"

"No, No! I didn't mean it like that. Sorry."

I laughed.

"It's okay. Just messing with you. Number one really that bad?" I asked.

At this, he faked a chill.

"Let's just say, I think she lied filling out her questionnaire in hopes of landing a certain kind of man. In the process, she got paired with me, and it was obvious from the beginning that we were not two people who should have been put together."

"I'm sorry to hear that. And just what kind of man was she looking to land that made her end up with you?"

He chuckled.

"Sane."

"Damn."

He shrugged again.

"Eh. It is what it is. Besides, it just narrows my options."

"But what if me and number three are also terrible? Then you have *no* options."

He looked over at me, and even though I couldn't see his eyes through the Koala's face, it felt like they were burning right through my mask to my own.

"I don't think I'll have to worry about that," he answered honestly. "I'm already having a much better time with you."

My cheeks flushed, and for once I was glad for this stupid panda mask. At least he couldn't see that his words had any kind of special effect on me.

I needed to remain calm and casual.

"Yes, well. That's all good and dandy, but what if I end this date not interested in *you*?"

"Ouch! But I'll give you that. I may bore you to death, or you'll find my terrible jokes, E.G. the dating other men one, to be off-putting."

"You're saying there's more?"

"Maybe."

"Do you always speak like you're a document rather than

a person?"

"The E.G?

"Yes."

"Only when I'm too lazy to actually say example given."

"That would still be weird, but at least now I've learned you're lazy."

He laughed again, much harder this time, and to be honest, I loved the sound of his soft laugh.

"I'm not lazy, per se. Not all of the time. Or often. *Rarely.* Throw me a ladder any time you're ready to help me out of this hole I'm digging."

"Okay, okay. I'll give you a break on this one."

"Thank you!"

He then pointed out that we had barely actually eaten any of our food, so we put most of the conversation on hold except for a few sparse comments and got to work chowing down. After all, there was still the rest of the date left after lunch, and I found myself quite looking forward to it.

A IS FOR AUGUST

AFTER LUNCH, WE headed to a nearby park that had a small playground, a water fountain, and a winding path lined with trees for people to walk or ride bikes along. In this case, we chose to walk. Mostly because neither of us randomly decided to come prepared with a bike, (You know, 'cuz ya never know when ya might need one), but also because it was too nice to pass up the opportunity to spend some time outside.

There was a light but warm breeze rustling the leaves in the trees, and the sounds of laughing, playing children all around. My mystery Koala man surprised me by reaching for my hand as we began our walk, and I surprise myself even more because I let him take it.

His hand was warm, but not the kind of warm that will leave your own sweaty after you let go. I didn't instantly feel the need to rub my hand on the skirt of my dress. (Or in a bottle of hand sanitizer. And I *have* before.) His hand was soft too, much softer than it looked, as I could see the signs of wear. Scars.

Callouses. It made me wonder what he must do to get them that way. How is his free time spent? What did he do for a living? If only I could ask.

"I like to come to this park often," he mentioned, pulling me back out of my drifting thoughts. "It's a nice place to walk Luna."

"I'm not sure if this is cheating, probably, but I will go ahead and assume that Luna is a dog. I mean, it's not really too odd of a guess. Most people don't walk their cats."

In his response, I could hear another smile. I only wished I could see it.

"Well, since you guessed and didn't ask, yes. Her name is Luna. She's a white and gray pit bull puppy with adorable, big, blue eyes. I've had her about four months now, and this is her favorite place."

"I have a bunny. Her name is Cinnabun. She's sandy colored and a little over a year old."

"Mutual animal lover. Good to know."

We walked around for a little while without really saying much, but it wasn't an awkward silence. It wasn't really a silence at all, considering all of the things to listen to around us. Our hands swung together as we walked.

We were nearing a pond in the park that was surrounded

by benches. He led me over to one and we both sat down, him stretching out beside me. There were ducks in the water, quacking and swimming around. We watched them for a moment.

"My name is Ella," I announced, breaking the silence. "I just wanted you to know that now. You don't have to waste one of your questions on it."

"Thanks. I appreciate you giving me a better question opportunity." He looked over at me, and I couldn't be sure what, exactly, he saw there. Was he looking at my panda mask, or imagining the face underneath? "My name is August."

"Like the month?"

(What else, Ella? What else?)

"Exactly like the month.

"That's... kinda neat. I like it."

"Thank you. I hope you might like this as well."

He reached into his pocket and pulled out a small box. (Smooth, August. Real Smooth.) It was plain, wrapped in brown paper like an old-fashioned parcel, and tied with thin, white string. He handed it to me and I carefully undid the little bow and eased the top off. What I found inside was not at all what I had been expecting. It was a single scrabble tile with the letter A printed on it in black and a subscript number one.

Confused, I raised an eyebrow (who knows why at this

point) and turned to him.

"A scrabble tile?"

"So you have something to remember me by. It's cheesy, maybe even a little lame, but... I feel like gifts that give a person something to remember you by, rather than simply an object they may or may not like, is more... meaningful. Does that make sense?"

I smiled. It made a lot of sense.

"Actually, I'd have to say I agree with you. Thank you. And congratulations. You've just earned yourself all three questions."

"I'm smiling right now," he said. "You just can't see it."

"Me too."

We stared into each other's animal eyes... somewhat... weirdly. Somewhat romantically, I suppose. I mean, it was supposed to be. I was sure of that.

"So... question number one. What habits do you have that tend to annoy other people?"

I laughed.

"Getting the bad out of the way first, huh?" I asked him.

"I mean, I'd like to know what I may be getting myself into," he answered honestly. "Wouldn't you?"

"I suppose. In that case, I'm a bit of a neat freak. Everything in our apartment has its own place. All of our cupboards in the kitchen are labeled. I categorize. Even our closets have to be in order. The only room I don't have control over is my sister's bedroom. Otherwise, I've even recently decided our bathroom needed rearranging, and she didn't like that."

I knew Ava had a problem with this, and our parents used to get on my case about it, mostly teasing me, but no one else had ever really known. I wondered if this would be something to scare someone away with. Worse yet, what if he was a slob?

"Interesting," was all that he responded with.

(Seriously, Dude?)

"Interesting in a good way, or a bad way?" I asked to try and clarify.

"Definitely not a bad way. I can't say I'm on your level, but I do like to consider myself neat, so I don't think I'd have a problem with it. As long as you'd be willing to be patient with someone and, say, not chew them out for forgetting to put something in its proper place."

"Oh, no chewing out. You're safe there."

"Good! Question two, then. What do you spend most of your free time doing? Besides organizing, obviously."

"Oh ha ha." I couldn't see if he was smiling, but I was fairly certain he had a shit-eating grin on his face right about then. I could almost feel it. "Reading, playing with Cinnabun, and I suppose binge-watching TV. It's kind of lame. I don't go out much or anything."

"It's not lame. It's you. I don't go out much either. I used to, at least a little more than I do now, but I don't know... life keeps me busy. So... third and final question, maybe of the day, maybe forever. I suppose I better make it count."

"Give me your best."

He thought for a long time while I watched the ducks some more. I wished I had something to feed them.

"What is your favorite thing about yourself, as a person, not physically?" he finally asked.

"Seriously?"

"Yes."

Part of me wondered why that was the third and final question he decided to ask. Part of me believed I was only wondering because I didn't want to have to answer it. What did I actually really like about myself? Why was that something I had to think so hard about?

I must have been quiet for too long. He looked over at me as if to check and see whether I was still there. I then wondered if it looked bad that I couldn't think of anything.

"Uh... I guess... I'm a good person."

"You *guess* you're a good person?"

"I mean I am. I'm a good person. I've never intentionally hurt anyone. I've never wanted to for that matter. I'd help people if they asked for it, even if I didn't know them. I wish I could do things to better this world. I guess I just... I have my flaws, but being a bad person isn't one of them."

He nodded along, and I couldn't tell what he was thinking, but I hoped that I made sense. One of my flaws was definitely not knowing how to explain myself very well. In my head, an award-winning novelist. In reality, a child learning to talk for the first time. That's how it felt, anyway.

"Alright!" he said abruptly, somewhat startling me. "I think I should let you get on with your day. After all, I've monopolized a good chunk of it by now. Also, my office is going to get peeved if I'm not back soon. I just took *the* longest lunch break of my career. What do you say?"

"Oh my, God! I didn't know you were on a lunch break!"

"Hey, it's not your fault. I've simply been enjoying my time with you and I let it get carried away. Would you like me to walk you back to the bus station? It's sort of far from here now, and what's a few more minutes for me?"

"I would like that. Thank you."

He stood up and offered me his hand, which I took

happily. He may not have had any sort of commentary for my third response, but I was still pretty sure that this date had been very successful. At least for me, August was in the lead.

Kelli Rajala

THE BAD AND THE GOOD

WHEN I GOT home, Ava wasn't there. It was unfortunate, because I wanted to tell her about my date. Also, I didn't go back to work until Thursday, so I didn't really have a lot to do. Eventually, I decided on cuddling up with Cinnabun and a book on our living room couch. I even propped the window open just enough to get a small breeze circulating through the room. It was wonderfully peaceful.

As I'd already stated when talking to August, reading was a big part of my 'me time.' Half of our living room was devoted to being part of my miniature library, with my absolute favorites being stored neatly on the shelves in my bedroom.

The book I was reading at that time wasn't my usual taste, but since I started the Dating Experiment, I thought maybe it would be interesting to pick up one of today's more popular Young Adult choices. It was a contemporary romance about a girl and a guy who grew up in very different social circles, but have found they have so much in common regardless. Honestly, it was such a cliche that I had already figured out how it was going to end before I even got halfway through.

About an hour or so later, Ava came barging through the door. Normally, this wouldn't be her style, so I knew immediately that something was up.

"Hey, what's going on?" I asked. "Is everything okay?"

She tossed her bag in the general direction of her bedroom and then came to plop down on the couch beside me.

"The date wasn't even over," is the response I got.

"Huh?"

"My date. I just went on a date and I couldn't even let it get to the end."

"That bad?"

"Worse!" She sighed and rubbed at the bridge of her nose. "This guy was the most arrogant, selfish, ungodly asshole I've ever been unfortunate enough to have to go on a date with!"

"Ouch... I'm really sorry to hear that. What happened exactly?"

She went on to explain how rude he was to everyone, including her. He was extremely condescending and treated her as though he thought that, as a woman, she was definitely beneath him. He even had the nerve to tell her that he didn't believe in getting the girls gifts on the first date, regardless of the fact that it was part of the game, so he didn't get her one. She'd get one if he picked her. Then, he talked about himself. A LOT.

"I practically had to listen to his whole life story, and when we got to his career? Oh my God, I couldn't handle it. He's the marketing manager for some... relatively well-off business. I don't know. I didn't pay that much attention, but he's in the six-figure range, so apparently, that makes him really important? He went on and on about all he does for his company, and how he runs things. The guy has no problem firing people for the dumbest of reasons!"

"Yikes... how did you get matched with him?"

"I don't know!" she practically yelled. "I was starting to wonder the same thing. If you ask me, this Dating Experiment is not as accurate as it says."

"Well... I'm not sure it's their fault," I admitted. "My date today swore the first woman he went out with lied on her questionnaire. If you really think about it, they can only be as accurate as we are honest. I'm sure he wouldn't have put all his negative traits as answers."

She sighed.

"I guess you're right. These things can't come without flaws if you're expecting everyone to be completely honest. I'm sorry I didn't even remember you went on a date, though. How was it?"

"It's okay. It went really well, actually. He was super nice, and we had some things in common. He was easy to talk to."

"That's great!"

There was a smile on her face, but I knew she was still thinking about the disaster that was her own second date. I could see the irritation in her eyes. She wanted to be there for me, but she also really wanted to bitch about this terrible guy she had met, and so I decided to keep things short.

"Yeah. It was. We went on a walk in the park and everything was so relaxed. It was fun. That's pretty much it, though. Nothing exciting. Your guy, on the other hand...."

And so I let her continue, and she picked up like there had never been a moment where she felt obligated to ask about me. The next things I learned? He doesn't believe in chivalry, because he's a feminist. (His words. Literally no one else's.) He thinks he's this good samaritan, charitable kind of guy, because one time a lady at the grocery store came up a dollar short and he paid the dollar for her. And let's not forget... he watches Fox News. (Enough said.)

-

Ava went in for a later shift starting at 4:00 P.M. That once again left me home alone with Cinnabun, so I decided to order some take-out for dinner at around 6:00. I got Chinese, because it's always been my ultimate favorite, and looked to see if there was anything interesting on Netflix. For some reason, I ended up watching a documentary about a serial killer, as if that's perfectly normal for someone to watch while they're home alone in the evening.

When my food finally arrived I spread it all out on our coffee table and took a little bit of everything. Admittedly, this dinner cost me $40.00 for just myself, but there would be plenty of leftovers to make up for it, as long as I sort of buried them in the refrigerator where Ava couldn't easily see the boxes. Not that I believed for one minute that she wouldn't be able to simply sniff them out regardless, but it was worth a try.

I was stuffing my face with sweet and sour chicken dripping with sauce when I noticed my phone light up out of the corner of my eye. I shoved the rest of the piece in, chewing awkwardly with my mouth open, because of how full my mouth was, and wiped away the gooey sauce that was now dripping down my chin with the nearest napkin. (Cute sight, I'm sure.)

It was August.

August: Hey there! Remember me?

The Dating Experiment

I hesitated a moment, staring at the text on the screen long enough to make sure that I was seeing it correctly. Of course I remembered him. We had only just been hanging out earlier that day, so why was he texting me? Was he allowed to be texting me?

Me: Of course. Is this legal, though? We're not officially dating.

Of course I asked, because simply answering him wouldn't have been a good enough response. It didn't take him long to respond. He must have been waiting.

August: There's nothing saying it's -not- legal.
Me: Fair point. What's up?
August: Not a whole lot. I just got off work a little bit ago. Now I'm watching TV by myself in my pajamas like a loser.
Me: Lol! I am too, though. So maybe I shouldn't laugh too hard at that.
August: :D We can be losers together. Don't worry.

My face lit up with the goofiest smile.

August: I had fun today. I just wanted to let you know that. Did I mention that earlier? I don't think I did. Anyway... now you know. So I guess... do with that what you will.

Aw. Could he be any cuter?

Me: I had fun too. Just so -you- know. :)

There was a small part of me that was ecstatic at that moment. I went on a date with a guy and it was fun. It went well. That hadn't happened in a really long time for me. Then there was the part of me that was suddenly very nervous. I went on a date with a guy... and it was fun. It... went well. That... hadn't happened in a really long time for me. I wasn't sure how to feel now that it was. I could barely remember what dating was actually like. Could it even be said that my ex and I had dated? It seemed to me more like we had been friends, and then just sort of fell into the whole boyfriend/girlfriend thing. Maybe I had never really known how to 'date' in the first place. Oh, God. What had I gotten myself into?

What if I made a fool of myself?

What if I fell in love and he didn't love me back?

What if *I* was the one who had to turn *him* down?

What if I ruined this?

-

Ava didn't get off work until 11:00 P.M. When she came through the door, she dropped her bags and slid down the door until she was sitting on the floor.

"How'd it go tonight?" I asked.

"I'm much more used to doing this during the day. The lunch shift is never this busy. I mean, on one hand, it's great, because my tips were awesome. However, I was soooo busy."

"Well, look at it this way. Whatever guy you end updating, you can just tell him to try and leave your days open. Go on mostly evening dates. That way you can keep your lunch shift."

She nodded.

"That's not a bad idea."

"Think about it. Meanwhile, I'm gonna head to bed. I just wanted to make sure you got in okay and everything."

She smiled.

"Thanks, sis. I appreciate when you wait up for me. You know you don't have to."

"I do know that. But I'm the worrier of the family, remember? I gotta make sure you get in. Otherwise, if you're so much as a minute late, I'll be forced to call the police and report you missing."

"Ha ha. Please don't ever do that."

"Okay. Sorry. Five minutes."

"Good night, Ella."

"Good night."

NO SPARKS WITH THE MOUSE

IT WAS THE morning of my third date. Today's man was to be a mouse. Honestly, I wasn't sure whether to be excited for this one or not. There was already something about August that sort of made me want to go on another date with him. Mr. Mouse was going to have to try real hard if he wanted to impress me.

"Do you want anything? I'm making breakfast."

Ava was in the kitchen. I could smell bacon wafting through the apartment, along with something mapley. My excitement peaked.

"Are you making french toast?"

"Yeah."

"Then yes!"

French toast = my favorite breakfast food of them all. The supreme breakfast essential. Not something to be passed up when offered. Plus, Ava used mom's recipe, and it was somehow even better than all other french toast. She honestly didn't even have to ask.

"Powdered sugar?"

"Uh, duh!"

I walked out into the living room and plopped down on the couch while I waited for Ava to be done cooking. For some reason, I hadn't mentioned that August had texted me last night, even though I'm sure she would have flown through the roof with excitement if she knew. I wondered, then, if I should mention it now.

I chose not to.

"Supposed to be a light breezy day today. Not quite as warm as the others," she said.

"I can't wait for fall weather. It's the best, honestly."

"Mm-hm."

Ava set a plate out for me before fixing one for herself, and we sat across from each other at our small, circular kitchen table, sipping glasses of orange juice between bites.

It was weird, in a way. For the past two days, we hadn't been seeing much of each other, and this was going to go on for the rest of the month. Usually, unless one of us was at work, or unless Ava was out with another one of her boyfriends, we were pretty much always together. It had been weird when I first moved in, but then it started to become more like we were back at home again as little kids. Just as close.

Now it was weird again.

Mostly for Ava, since I was always the one being a hermit in our apartment. I was used to Ava leaving often, but Ava wasn't used to *me* leaving for anything other than short work shifts.

"I feel like I'm not invested enough in your experience," she casually commented.

"What do you mean?" I asked.

"Well, I got you into this whole thing, yet I haven't really talked to you much about it. I mean, sure, there's the dates and all that, but what's it like doing things you don't normally do? Going places you normally don't go? Meeting other people in general?"

I shrugged.

"It's okay... I guess. I didn't really put much thought into it."

"So put some thought into it now."

"Yeah. Okay. I guess it was nice talking to this girl I met on the bus my first day. Her name was Katie. She seemed cool. I kind of hope we run into each other again. And I'm getting more comfortable taking the bus to all these different places. Not just to the bakery. It's fun. All of it... it's all fun."

"I'm really glad to hear that, Ella. I was hoping this would be a good experience for you overall."

"Uh huh. Thanks, Mom."

She rolled her eyes at that.

A little while after breakfast was over I got another text, this time from my date tonight.

[Mouse]: Good morning! I hope you've had a lovely start to your day, thus far! I've made reservations for two at The Bronze Tower for 5 p.m. tonight. I look forward to seeing you there.

(A long date ensued.)

I'll refrain from all of the fluff that was this third date and say this: It was perfect. It was the date every young girl dreams of going on at some point in her lifetime. First of all, The Bronze Tower is a high-end restaurant, the kind where you need a reservation and you *must* be dressed in your best. I got to wear a sparkly, black, cocktail dress with killer high heels.

The Bronze Tower is also exactly what it sounds like. It's a shiny bronze building with fifty floors. The food is amazing, but a budget breaker for most people. I wondered what Mr. Mouse, whose name I eventually learned was Joshua (NOT Josh), must have done for a living if he was willing to fork out so much cash on women he may have never seen again.

When I arrived at the station, he was waiting for me at the exit, and we walked arm in arm to the restaurant. There, he ordered a bottle of wine for our table and a chicken dinner with roasted vegetables. We split a chocolate lava cake for dessert and it had that orgasm-in-your-mouth warm, melted goodness that only could have been created by a god/goddess.

For the event part of the date, we went and saw a romantic comedy in theaters that he swore he hadn't seen two times already, though I'm pretty sure I caught him whispering along to the funnier bits.

For the gift, he brought me a beautiful bouquet of pink and red roses that I put on our coffee table in the living room, so that they would be on display for anyone who walked into our apartment. It also gave them ample sunlight, given the large window lighting up the space. Even Ava was impressed by the flowers and, apparently, a little jealous. The bouquet she had received was a little on the skimpier side in comparison.

Of course, that didn't matter to me at the end of the day. In fact, nothing about this perfect date really mattered much to me. The man was a complete gentleman, opening up doors for me and pulling out chairs. He gave me his jacket when the wind got a little chilly, and our conversation flowed smoothly. I'd love to say he was the winning man, but...

I just didn't feel anything.

Maybe it was the fact that it was perfect. Too perfect. Like... it wasn't original enough, because he was trying too hard? He literally went with every young girl's fantasy date, which wasn't saying anything about his dates as individuals. He hadn't tried to figure out what I might like. He just figured out what a generic 20-something-year-old female would like.

Plus, though our conversation flowed smoothly, and though he was generally nice to talk to, there was nothing more to it than two people having a polite conversation. He could have talked the same way with someone he sat next to on a particularly long bus ride.

There were just no sparks.

Had there been with August? I'm not sure. But there was at least *some*thing.

"Well, I know who I'm picking," Ava announced as she sat next to me on the couch that night going over her options. "Number three was nice, and I had fun, but number one was unlike any man I've dated thus far, and I'm pretty sure that's exactly what I'm looking for."

"Agreed. I think I'm going to pick number two," I told her. "August."

"It's a shame you're not going with date number three. He sounds like every girl's dream."

I shrugged.

"I don't want every girl's dream, though. I want *my* dream."

Ava put down her list and looked at me, staring me up and down for just a moment.

"Shit," she finally said. "I'm not sure more wise words have ever been spoken."

I rolled my eyes, but smiled at the same time. I wouldn't call my words wise, just... true. I didn't want a guy who was a good match for 90% of the female population. I wanted a guy who was a good match for me. Wasn't that, like, kind of the whole point of this thing?

Now all I had to do was hope that August had picked me too. That would guarantee that we would be paired together the next day when we submitted our rankings.

MATCHES ARE MADE

WE ALL WENT back to the Center, because mailing things in would be too complicated and slow. Apparently. Not that staring at each other while someone sorts our matches by hand is going to feel any less slow, but it was already decided that that was the best plan of action. So there I sat, with Ava, Katie (who I'd reconnected with), and Ava's new friend, a skunk named Klare.

We handed ouu slips to a lady at the front desk. Then we were ushered into the middle room. There was a lot of buzz going around as people made guesses on whether or not they would be matched with their number one pick or not. Personally, I didn't want to be included in any of those conversations. I was too nervous already, imaging August had some amazing, practically-marriage-worthy date with his third woman.

"That guy in the mouse head is eyeing you up," Katie observed. "You must have made quite the impression."

She subtly pointed in his direction and I did my best to make it look like I was simply glancing around the room for general purposes. She was right. He wasn't looking in any other direction. He was looking directly at me. Whispering things to his buddy.

"We had a pretty good date," I admitted.

"Ooh! Is he your number one? Because I'm pretty sure you're his."

I shifted uncomfortably.

"Well... no... actually. The date was great, and he seemed like a really nice guy, but I feel like I connected with someone else."

Speaking of which, I did another casual sweep around the room and found August on the other end of our row. His eyes were not on me, though. They were on the skunk animatedly chatting away with my sister. That had to be his third date. There was no other reason I could think of for him to be watching her so intently. My first choice's eyes were on my sister's new friend. What if he picked her? That would be... awkward.

Maybe it did go well after all.

Maybe he wanted her.

"Ella?"

"Huh?"

I looked back at Katie, who was staring at me, her deer head looking just as lost as she probably was underneath it.

"Do you think you'll get paired with him?"

"I sure hope so."

Holly Van Warden walked into the room at that moment, her high heels clicking against the tile floor. She stood at her podium and addressed us all with a smile.

"Good morning, everyone! I hope this experience has been going well for all of you so far. As you know, today is the day where you ranked your dates from three being the worst to one being the best, and my team just got done sorting out the best-matched pairs!"

I'm not sure if we were supposed to cheer for that? Anyway, once the small awkward pause was out of the way, she continued...

"On the screen behind me, you will soon see who you got paired with. As always, we did our best and we sincerely hope that each choice we've made is just right for each and every one of you."

She stepped down out of the way and soon the screen on the wall behind her podium lit up. On it, appeared the female list, and after a dramatic pause (of course) the men's animal head pictures started to file in alongside the women's.

Across the room, I heard a lot of sighs of relief, and a few exclamations of joy. I belonged to the group of sighers once I saw August's koala face pop up next to my panda. I hoped that meant he picked me as his number one as well. There were good odds for that, right?

When I glanced over at him he was walking in my direction. I didn't even look to see who Ava got, whether or not it was the dream man from her first date. I was too focused on August, who came and stood in front of me and, though I still couldn't tell if he was smiling or not, I wanted to believe that he was. *I* was.

"Hey!" he said cheerfully.

"Hey. I see we will, in fact, be going on more dates."

"That we will, and I very much look forward to it."

"Oh... so did... I mean..."

"She was nice," he answered without me needing to finish the question. "The date was nice. However, my gut feeling told me that I should stick with the panda. She did seem pretty chill and all that, as far as pandas go."

My cheeks flushed.

"You're silly, but thank you. I'm glad you picked me."

I was very glad. I already liked hearing his voice again. God, maybe Ava was right. I had gone too long without a man in my life. I was desperate for a man's voice after one date! I had forgotten what I was missing, especially how it felt to have butterflies fluttering around inside my stomach.

We stood around talking for a while. I introduced him to Ava and she, in turn, introduced me to Nate. He was, luckily for her, the first-night-boat-guy. When we were done we said our goodbyes for the day, as there was no required date to go on. This meant *I* got to go into work.

-

I arrived at Sugar Beat ten minutes early to my late afternoon shift and got myself ready. My boss, Shannon, was covered in flour and putting the finishing details on a four-tier wedding cake. Honestly, those were the kinds of projects I wasn't allowed to touch yet. There was Shannon and her main crew, and then there were those of us who decorated children's birthday sheet cakes and cookies.

"Nice to see you again!" said Shannon. "I think this is the longest we've been without you."

"Shannon, it's only been three days."

She smiled.

"Yes, but you're one of my most reliable workers."

"That's because I usually don't have a life."

She laughed her sweet, soft laugh and shook her head.

"I suppose that works out well for me, now doesn't it? How's this whole, having a life thing working out anyway? Meet the man of your dreams yet?"

Unfortunately, I couldn't save myself the embarrassment of having to be honest to Shannon about why I needed days off. So yeah... she knew it all.

"I met a nice guy. I'm not sure he's the man of my dreams, though. We've only been on one date."

"Sometimes that's all it takes, Hon."

I couldn't help but roll my eyes. Shannon was a middle-aged hopeless romantic. We had very different views on the matter.

"You know I don't believe in that whole 'love at first sight' thing, right?" I asked.

She let out a defiant "hmpf!"

Meanwhile, I got to work. At this point in the day, I didn't get to do my usual decorating. Instead, I had to cover the front counter. I didn't mind the sales part, but my passions laid more in creating art with sugar and frosting. Sometimes with fondant, but in my personal opinion, that stuff mostly tastes like cardboard. (It *can* be pretty, though, and neater detail-wise... so we use it a lot.

At the time, since it was still officially summer, there were some warm weather themed cookies that I was particularly proud of. For instance, the beach ball, the popsicle, and the watermelon slice cookies. In my absence, they were made by the hands of someone else, but the designs were still mine.

I sold a family a pack of four cookies, which their son and daughter just *had* to have. The girl's favorite was the monarch butterfly cookie. That one was a favorite of mine as well. It always made me happy to do something for a living that not only made use of my creativity, but put such big smiles on the faces of our customers. I couldn't wait to have my own bakery. (If I could ever muster up what it took to open one.)

When the last few customers had gone about the rest of their day with the box of muffins I'd packaged for them, I grabbed our cleaning supplies out of the closet and got to tidying up the storefront. It never really got too dirty, but I took extra care in my work anyway, utilizing every last minute I was scheduled for.

After all was said and done, I closed up, said goodbye to Shannon, and left with a smile on my face. Overall, I'd had a productive and rather good day.

Tomorrow was the first date *I* would be planning. I was nervous about messing everything up, but underneath all of the questions running through my head as I made plans, was the comforting fact that August had picked me too. Maybe I needed to keep that more in the forefront of my mind.

A SOCCER TEAM OF CHILDREN

I WAS UP all night trying to figure out what to get August for his first gift. The date part was actually easy, because I picked something that people, in general, tended to really like. I know! I judged a guy for that earlier on. I'm a hypocrite, okay? But seriously, who doesn't like mini golf? (If it's you, shame on you... kidding! Sort of.)

I finally decided to get him chocolate. Guys always get girls chocolate, but who's to say men don't want it too? I even got him Dove brand chocolate, because, in my humble opinion, they make the very best! It's so smooth and creamy. *#getyourshittogetherotherchocolatecompanies. #sorrynotsorry.*

Anyway, we were going to get tacos for lunch. There was this taco truck that always parked in various places around town, all depending on what day of the week it was, and that Friday it happened to be relatively close to the mini-golf park. I did hope he liked tacos. That seemed like another general thing you'd have to be weird not to like. He had to like tacos.

I met up with August once I stepped off the bus. He was wearing a dark red button down with the sleeves rolled up. Why did guys always look so much more attractive with their sleeves rolled up? Doesn't matter who he is. He rolls up the sleeves of his collared oxford shirt and BAM! Hot. I wondered, briefly, if there was something that women could do that would have the same effect. What if we rolled *our* shirtsleeves up? Guys, can women achieve this level of instant hot as well? Asking for a friend...

"Hey, you!"

He waved as I walked up to the mini-golf park. It was a sunny and warm day, so there were a good number of people already there, scattered about the holes. August signed us in. I picked a pink ball. He picked one the color of a yellow highlighter. You know, the super bright would-hurt-your-eyes-if-there-was-too-much-of-it yellow. Then we headed to hole one.

I should have considered the fact that I sucked at mini golf before picking this place. It took me ten shots to get it into hole one! In fact, another group came in after us and I sort of held them up. August did good, though. He got it in two, which was par.

"I think you just need to readjust some more," he said, coming up behind me.

He did the thing that guys do, where they stand behind

you, wrap their arms around you, and guide your swing by holding on to your hands. Except he did it more awkwardly, because the animal heads were sort of getting in the way. I actually blamed them for my lack of ability. Couldn't see properly. That was all.

"You just did that so you could violate my personal space," I replied with a laugh.

"Oh, come on. You can't tell me you didn't have that classic move in mind when you picked this activity."

"I did not. Honestly."

(Honestly!)

I did better on hole two.

"See? I helped!"

He seemed so genuinely happy that I couldn't *not* smile.

"You may be right about that. Maybe you should consider helping me again. Then I might get a hole in one."

He chuckled lightly.

"I don't know about that. I wouldn't want to make you better than me."

"Ha! Right!"

We continued playing and, for the rest of the holes, I didn't do nearly as bad as the first one. There was some water on hole eight that tripped me up, but that one only took four shots.

There was also this really cool cave-like structure that we had to go into for one hole, and it got my feet all wet, but it was still fun.

There was no club slipping from our hands, or almost hitting someone with a stray ball. Regardless of my improving ability, though, August beat me by a fairly decent sized lead. We went around twice, just so I could try to beat him. Sadly, that didn't happen, but our scores were much closer together the second time around.

"Congratulations! Here is your prize!" I announced, handing him the candy bar I had stashed in my bag.

He laughed.

"Is this the gift you're supposed to give me regardless of whether I won or not?"

"Uh... yes, but it's even better now, because it's also a prize."

He nodded.

"You know what? I'll take that. Thank you!"

I pocketed my scorecard, we returned our balls and clubs, and then we took a leisurely walk to the taco truck. Thankfully, August did like tacos.

"Should we sit somewhere and eat?" he asked.

I nodded.

"There were benches back at the park. I'm sure they

wouldn't mind if we sat there for a little while."

And so we made our way back.

"Alright!" he said when we were sitting back down at one of those wooden, picnic bench style tables. "You've earned all three of your questions. You may ask me my deepest, darkest secrets now."

I laughed. Then I realized I hadn't really thought this part out enough. I was too busy trying not to plan a sucky date. I had to sit and think a while, though he didn't seem to mind.

"Ooh! I got one. If you won the lottery, would you still keep your job?"

"Absolutely."

"Really? How come?"

He turned to face me and leaned against the table.

"I love what I do. It makes me happy. And so you don't have to waste a question on it, I'm a veterinarian. And I think a good chunk of my money I would give to our local clinics and shelters."

"Now I see why my liking animals was so important to you."

"It was a must if I'm being honest."

"Understandable. Question two. What is your favorite book?"

"I feel like this is actually a question I can get terribly wrong if I pick a dumb one."

"Oh, I'll simply hard-core judge you for the rest of eternity, that's all."

He laughed and looked around.

"Hmm... That's all, huh? Ok then, I guess it would have to be... *Wicked*, by Gregory Maguire. Animal rights. Quirkiness. Seeing another side to someone you thought you knew. It has all the good stuff."

"Not a bad choice, actually. It's pretty far up on my list as well. Question three, then." (And I couldn't believe I was going to ask this, but I needed to know. Nearing 30 and all.) "Do... uh... would... you like children of your own someday? S-sorry... typical female question I suppose."

He sucked in a large breath and let it out slowly.

"No, that's not a bad question, though. I guess... I guess I would. I mean, I know I do. That's... that's another part of why I'm here. Maybe that sounds completely lame, I don't know, but... I'm not getting any younger. I'd like to find someone serious, someone I may spend the rest of my life with, someone else looking to settle down and start a family."

"That's not lame at all," I assured him. "I'm not getting any younger either, and I'm the one who eventually won't be able to have children. So... I'd like to find the same thing."

We both sat silently for a few moments, watching the other golfers in the park and finishing up our tacos. Finally, August broke that silence.

"I'm really glad we're on the same page about that."

"Me too."

"Next time we're allowed to ask each other questions we'll have to make sure that we're on the same page about the number." He laughed. "I don't want a whole soccer team worth of children. Just so you know."

"Yikes! I mean, I don't either! I don't think we have to worry about that."

He laughed again.

"Good, because some women want that."

"Gonna go out on a limb here and say you've dated one of them."

He nodded.

"It was a deciding factor in our breakup."

"I think you and I will be much more on the same page about that matter," I admitted.

"Me too. Meeee too."

He reached over and took hold of my hand. I laced my fingers through his. Our hands fit together well. I liked that. It wasn't all awkward and uncomfortable to hold his hand. We stayed like that for a long time, casually discussing random thoughts and ideas. It was a good date. I did well.

QUESTIONS AND MORE QUESTIONS

THINGS WERE GOING well with me and August. We each only missed one point in the next week. He learned that I don't like chili, or anything even remotely spicy for that matter. I learned that he sucked at planting literally anything. No green thumb there. I hadn't really expected him to be a plant aficionado, but part of me was hoping the wear and tear on his hands came from at least some landscaping ability. Guess I would be hiring someone for that job when I finally bought my own home.

As far as biggest wins go, his was Chinese take-out. The best! My all-time favorite! (As we should all already know.) Mine was the mini bottles of whiskey I gave him on our baking date. He didn't drink often, mostly when out with friends, but now he said he could sneak in his own and not have to pay the hefty price at a bar. That wasn't my intention with that gift, but I wasn't going to stop him. I just laughed.

A week from the mini golf game he took me to karaoke night. I'm not going to lie. I was up in the air for a while on whether I'd give him a point. However, even though I was terribly embarrassed and nervous and sort of hating him at the get-go, it actually turned out to be really fun! He wasn't that great either, so I got to laugh harder that night than I could remember laughing in a long time. We made a "great" duo.

As we were at the zoo, feeding the animals that Monday:

"What is your biggest fear?"

"No judging?" I asked.

"No judging," he promised.

"Dying. And not like... in the sense that nobody wants to. It's more about what comes after. What if there's nothing? What if... our consciousness still exists somewhere, but there's nothing there? It's just an empty void, and that's where we're stuck, because we don't come back like we want to, as a new person. What if our souls are just all floating around, lost forever?"

He was quiet for a long time. He never acknowledged the response, formally, only nodded.

(Maybe that was a tad too dark?)

"What would you say your biggest weaknesses are?" he asked next.

"I don't put myself out into the world enough. What you're witnessing this month? It's not me. Not usually. I haven't made so much as a friend in... years. And since moving in with my sister it's just been the two of us. I'm hard on myself. Often. Sometimes it's like I can't always see that what I'm doing is good enough."

"What makes you proud of yourself?"

"I'm a good bunny mom. I've been successful so far in life with school and now my work. I had the courage to join this game. I'm making a decent life for myself."

At our picnic on Tuesday. My questions this time:

"What are three specific things that bring you joy?"

"Easy! My dog, other people's dogs, and dogs that may not belong to anyone, but they're still dogs."

"August!"

"Okay, okay. My dog *is* one, though. Also... warm, sunny days and biking."

"Biking?"

"Sure. I do it often in my free time. It's exercise, but it's fun. Plus, I go all over the city and see all sorts of people and things. If I'm not taking Luna with me, I'm on my bike."

"How would you describe your family?"

"Just my mom, dad, and me. My parents have always been great. They were a little strict from time to time, and they made me work for everything I wanted, even as a child, but I think because of that I'm a better person. I like who I am, and they're responsible for raising me, so kudos to them. We still keep in touch these days, spend holidays and all that together. They're good people."

"I'd say my family was relatively the same," I added. "Except most of them making us work for things was because they simply couldn't hand us what we wanted for free, even if that was something they wanted to do. We weren't wealthy, by any means. But I never resented that."

"It helps you stay humble."

"Exactly."

And on Wednesday, which was people watching and Chinese take-out day:

"Are you a morning or a night person?" he asked

"Neither! I like the middle of the day. Early to bed, late to rise. That's me."

He laughed at that one.

"How do you relieve stress?"

"I read, or I play with Cinnabun. If things are really stressful, though, like... I can't sit still long enough to read, or Cinnabun isn't helping, I bake. It's a science and an art, something that requires a good deal of concentration. Plus, the results taste amazing!"

"Yeah, books taste sort of like paper, and eating Cinnabun

would just be bad all around."

"Oh my, God!"

"It's true!"

"Yes, but you didn't need to go there!"

His ensuing laugh was contagious.

"Alright. Final question this time around. Is it easy or hard for you to express your feelings to people?"

"Ooh... that depends," I answered honestly. "I suppose it's very easy if I know the person well enough. Like, if we're super close you're going to hear about everything whether you want to or not. Typically, though, I have a hard time opening up to most people. It takes me a while to feel that level of comfort. Some people are open books with everyone. I'm definitely not one of those people."

Thursday, the last day I had been able to ask him all three questions:

"Okay now, this one is super important," I warned him. "Could even be a deal breaker. Are you ready?"

"Oh no... give me a moment." Long pause. "Okay. I think I'm ready."

"Do you sleep with your bedroom on the cold or the warm side."

"You're right. This could be a dealbreaker. My final

answer is (SUPER dramatic pause) cold."

"Correct!"

We laughed like fools here because, you know, that's just what you do.

"Give me a weird, but fun fact about yourself."

"That's not even technically a question."

"So? Go for it."

"Okay. Um... This might sound extremely dumb, but I can eyebrow dance?"

"Um. What? I believe you need to show me this immediately after we're allowed to take these masks off. Until then I just have to take your word."

"You got it. What else?"

"What do you like most about this city?"

He thought about this one for a while.

"It's the kind of place I've always wanted to live. I grew up in a smaller city. It wasn't bad, but I wanted more. The nice thing about here is that it's not too big either. I could never move to NYC. It's fun to visit, but exhausting after about a week. Here? You still have a sense of community with those around you, and yet there's still so much to do."

"A very good answer. I would have to agree with you on all points."

The Dating Experiment

In our more relaxed moments, when we weren't asking questions or partaking in activities, we'd simply sit together, either holding hands or me leaning into him with his arm around me. We gave each other hugs now when we first got together. There was something to be said about physical contact. Talking was great, especially with all the deep questions, but once we stopped being too afraid to actually touch each other, our connection grew that much stronger. I definitely liked him a lot.

Things were going well for Ava too, as far as I knew. Nate took her on some pretty amazing dates from what she told me, and his gifts were usually very pretty and thoughtful. She didn't talk about it all as much as I expected her to, but she willingly listened to every detail I had about my own experiences. She also seemed happy that this was working out so well for me. I was too. I was glad she had managed to talk me into it after all.

DANCING AND SWEAT

THE EVENT CENTER offered dance classes every Friday for those who weren't sure their skills would cut it for the reveal ball. The Friday of my karaoke date with August, I first went to dance class with Ava, Klare, and Katie. Dancing was probably my least favorite thing to attempt to do ever, so I was glad that it was only us plus two other women.

Surprisingly, though, we had professional male dancers to partner up with. I guess it made sense, because we were allowed to go to this optional event without the masks on, but I was still a little shocked to see six tall men in body tight clothing half gliding into to the room. Of course, this caused a bit of giggling from some of the others.

Our instructor was a large French woman that none of us could understand very well. She came in with an old boombox that played crappy quality waltz music, and was a surprisingly strict woman. Nonetheless, it was actually pretty fun.

I don't think it would take a genius to figure out that I

hated dancing because I was bad at it. My poor partner. I could only imagine he came into that session like he did every Friday, energized and ready to go. Then he met me. I stepped on his feet about 300 times in one session and suddenly he wanted off of that dance floor.

Ava, Klare, and Katie thought this was hilarious. They were laughing up a storm at my lack of coordination. I actually tripped over my partner's feet once and, when I ultimately hit the floor, I took him down with me. Our instructor looked like she was about to faint, and fanned herself excessively. She seemed okay once he got back up, but she looked at me like I was a piece of animal dung sticking to the bottom of someone's shoe.

We took a break about an hour in, where we were allowed to go to the bathroom and get water. I was already exhausted and wishing for the whole thing to be over with already. Then I remembered... I was going to have to dance with August if all went well. I couldn't let him experience this. The thought struck me with horror! And that meant I was going to have to get back out there and give this my all if I wanted to learn.

"There was another girl here last week who wasn't much better," Klare assured me.

"Thanks... I guess."

"You could always fake a broken leg or something, come

the reveal ball," was Ava's wise decision.

It wasn't actually all that bad of an idea. Maybe just a sprain would do it. That wouldn't be as hard to fake.

"One of us could learn the male role," Katie threw in. "You know, so you could practice with us outside of Friday classes. I'd be willing."

That was an even better idea.

"You'd really do that for me?"

She nodded.

"Totally! I mean, we're not competing or anything. We're all in this together, hoping that it works out for at least one or two couples, right?"

One or two couples? Were those the actual odds of this experiment? If so, that was kind of sad.

"Right," I agreed. "Thank you then. I really appreciate it."

"Not a problem. I'll go over right now and talk to our instructor. I'm sure she won't mind, I mean... she's seen you dance."

"Gee... thanks."

Ava and Klare laughed while Katie practically skipped over to the other side of the room where our instructor was busy chatting up the male dancers. The fact that she had to be in her mid to late fifties when they were all in their twenties didn't seem to be a problem as she flirted with each and every one of them. At least *she* was having fun.

Ava came up behind me and pulled me into a hug.

"I'm sorry. I didn't know you were this bad at dancing when I sighed us up for the Dating Experiment."

"None of you are helping with your comments."

Klare chuckled. I rolled my eyes and then took another long sip of my bottled water, even though it was gross. I hated chilled water, as picky as that was. Only room temperature for this girl.

Katie came back over with both thumbs up.

"She said that I'm doing well in the female spot, so it would be alright if I took the next half of our lesson to work on the male part for you."

"Great!"

Did I improve for the second round? No. Was Katie going to regret agreeing to help me? Probably. Did that stop her from being enthusiastic about it? Surprisingly, not a bit. I hoped that we'd continue this budding friendship once the month was up. She seemed like someone I would definitely like to keep around.

-

Anyway, enough of that mess. Monday morning August and I decided to try an early morning badminton workout, since both of us had to be into work that afternoon. I made us pulled pork sandwiches for lunch. Though, sadly, the pulled pork came out of an aluminum tub I'd pulled out of our freezer, because there was no way I was going to successfully cook that pork otherwise. He seemed to like them regardless. So that was a win.

Thankfully, I was much better at badminton than I was at dancing, even with the panda head. My sister and I used to play all the time when we were kids, usually with our parents, but sometimes by ourselves, because our parents were bad and kind of got in the way a lot. Me and Ava, though, we always joked that we could have made it to the Olympics. (Maybe we should have explored that more. Just for fun.)

August wasn't bad either. He made a very worthy opponent. I still beat him, but he put up a real fight.

Oh! before I forget. Don't worry! These animal heads were made to prevent us from killing ourselves by overheating. I don't know exactly what they were made of, but it was very breathable, whatever it was. And the ventilation was good. Props to the D.E. runners for thinking of such a potential issue. Though, I suppose you think of *every*thing if you don't want to get sued.

"I wouldn't have guessed you were so athletic," he commented as I sprinted to the other side of the net to catch a shot he purposefully aimed far away from me.

"I'm not," I said. "Not usually. This is about the only sport I'm able to kick ass at. Why? Do I look that out of shape?"

"No! Of course not. Not how I meant that. Kicking ass, though, that is exactly what you're doing. I think you brought me here this morning to try and kill me!"

I laughed.

"I promise that's not the case. But hey, you're doing well!"

"I mean, I've played some mean badminton back in the day, but not on this level. I only *thought* I was good, apparently."

We were at a public court, so other people were watching. It was funny. There were a few people who had stopped their own games to sit on the sidelines and watch. Eventually, we had fans. Some rooting for me, some rooting for August. More rooting for me, because clearly, I was the one dominating.

When it was getting close to the time we needed to head out, we stopped to eat. Our spectators went about their business, while I pulled the container of pulled pork out of my mini cooler. There was a little room off to the side with vending machines, water fountains, and a small kitchenette. I microwaved the pork and came back out to find August sprawled out of the ground by our things.

"Here, eat," I said. "Food will help."

I handed him the container and the bag of burger buns I had also brought.

We talked while we ate. I gave him is present, which was a handmade card I had whipped up the night before. I got to ask all three of my questions, and then we just laid there. On the ground. Next to each other.

I felt like I was going to need a shower before I went into work. My clothes were soaked through with sweat. I'm sure I smelled pretty rank too. It was hard to tell with the panda head, though. There was still a hint of whatever cleaning solution they had used on them masking everything else around me.

Did August care that we were gross, however? No.

"Hey, come here."

"Huh?"

"Come here."

I rolled over onto my side to look at him. He was watching me. I felt an arm loop around my side from underneath, and then, before I knew what was actually happening, he pulled and rolled me over so that I was lying on top of him.

"Ew! Gross, we're all sweaty!" I complained, trying to push away.

"It doesn't bother me," he said.

So I tried not to let it bother me either as I laid the panda head down on his chest and let him hold me in his arms.

SISTERLY SURPRISE

I'M SO GLAD our next activities were much calmer. The last few really wore me out. That Tuesday, we watched a cute romantic comedy, which I knew he only picked because he wanted me to like it. (Smart choice, August.) Wednesday we went to the museum and spent all afternoon visiting every one of the exhibits for at least a few minutes. Interestingly, it was way bigger than I thought (that's what she said?), and we almost got lost trying to find our way back out.

Thursday was my favorite day. He took me to an animal shelter to volunteer, and let's just say he clearly hadn't thought the whole thing out beforehand.

"I swear, if I'd realized sooner that we would be put on poop scoop duty, I would have rearranged for a more romantic date."

I cracked up. I couldn't help it. Poor August.

"What? You mean the overpowering smell of cat urine isn't a turn on for you too?"

And now he cracked up. And I was positive we both looked hysterical. See? You can make the best out of any situation, even if that situation finds you scooping up poop on what is supposed to be a romantic date with the girl/guy you really like.

"Do I still get a point for this?"

"Of course. You tried. How were you supposed to know that our large panda and koala heads would scare the animals half to death? It's not like most animals are naturally skittish or anything."

"You can't see it right now, but I am rolling my eyes so hard."

"Careful," I warner. "I may take away a point for that."

So, after spending the day scooping poop, cleaning cages, dusting, washing food dishes, and generally getting all up in the grime of the animal shelter, we shed our dirty work gloves and I invited him back to our apartment so he could clean up a bit.

After a brief discussion on food, he decided that we would eat there too, but that he would be the one to cook, since this was his date after all. We settled on some good, old-fashioned Kraft Macaroni and Cheese and called it a deal.

Now, if you're thinking that things could have gone better date wise, hold onto your seat, because they were about to get a whole lot more interesting at the after party.

Little did I know that upon returning to our apartment, August and I wouldn't be alone. I thought that Ava was out on a date with Nate, because that *is* what she told me, after all. And why would she need to lie to me? Turns out that was a cover story, and she had quite the reason to lie.

So we walked into the apartment and already I was like, okay, why are there lights on? *We* pay the electric, Ava! But I ignored that shortly after and instead focus on directing August to our bathroom. He made a few comments on how organized and clean everything was, and I joked that I had warned him.

Once he was in the bathroom, I set my bag down and kicked off my shoes. I was about to fall into the couch when I noticed the glow coming from underneath Ava's bedroom door. Obviously, I had to investigate. I know what you're thinking at this point. I'm about to walk in on Ava and Nate gettin' it on, right? Wrong!

Ava wasn't gettin' it on with Nate. Ava was gettin' it on with *Klare*!

After peeking in to see what was going on, I slowly attempted to back out and retreat to the living room where I would grab August once he came out of the bathroom and hastily drag him out of our apartment. Unfortunately, I stumbled and smacked into the door frame, causing both Ava and Klare to repel from each other like two positive ends of a magnet. The shock and horror on Ava's face was priceless, while Klare looked like this was an everyday event for her. I sure hoped it wasn't.

"Ella!"

"D-don't worry," I said, still trying to back out. "I-I'm just gonna go."

"We should talk about this!" she argued. "This isn't how I wanted you to find out."

"Yeah. Sure. Later, okay?"

"Ella, please!"

I shut the door and went to grab my shoes. By now, August was just stepping out of the bathroom.

"We're going!" I said abruptly, grabbing his hand.

"Wait, what's wrong?" he asked.

At the end of his question, Klare came stumbling out of Ava's bedroom, half dressed, half holding the rest of her clothes to her body. August froze.

"No, please!" I said to Klare. "Don't stop on my account. You and my sister were here first."

I heard the smallest "oh" come from beside me, where August was still glued to his spot on the floor.

"No. It's alright," Klare assured me. "I shouldn't be here right now. I swear I didn't know she didn't... well, I thought you knew."

"Well I didn't!"

It was then that August finally moved, turning to face me.

"Hey, I think maybe I should go too."

"What? Why?"

He put his hands on my shoulders and pulled me into a hug, but I didn't return it.

"I think you and your sister need to sit down and have a conversation. It wouldn't be right of me to stay. It's personal, after all. I'll take the loss of points and make it up to you on Saturday."

I knew he was right, but I really didn't want him to leave. Or, I suppose, I wanted to leave with him.

"Yeah... okay."

Klare snuck out the door as August squeezed me tighter. I leaned into him, sighing, realizing for the first time that I could smell wood and earthy spices when I breathed him in, barely noticeable over the interior of the panda mask. I closed my now watering eyes and finally wrapped my arms around him in return.

Then he let go.

I watched him leave. I listened to the door click shut. And then I stood in silence. Ava could be heard sniffling from her bedroom, with its door cracked open from Klare's departure.

I know what it looked like, on my part, at least to Ava and

maybe Klare. It looked like I was upset at the fact that my sister was hooking up with another woman. It wasn't that, though. I was upset because she hadn't told me about it. There was no indication of her being interested in women. And at that moment, all I could think was that she must not have trusted me enough to share that with me.

Was I being selfish? Most definitely. After all, this was something *she* was going through, and really, it was her life that was changing from it all. Maybe she was confused. Maybe this was scary for her. I didn't know, because all I could do was stand there and cry, wondering what I may have done to make my own sister think she couldn't come to me.

I thought we were close. Closer than ever.

I did finally (wo)man up about the whole thing and sneak back into Ava's room sometime later. She was sitting up now, wrapped in her fuzzy, lavender bathrobe. Her mascara was running down her cheeks and, when she looked up at me, all I could see was pain. Whether or not it was directed at me, it was hard to tell. Either way, I didn't like it.

I climbed into bed next to her, ignoring what had been going on in that same bed just moments ago, and wrapped her in a hug. She leaned on my shoulder. We didn't talk for a long time. We just sat there, giving each other comfort as best as we could manage. The rest of our apartment building seemed either asleep or away, because the quiet that surrounded us was almost deafening. At the same time, it was peaceful. Too many conflicting feelings and emotions were in the air and inside of us.

But at the end of the day, she was my sister... and I was going to love her no matter what.

NON-AWKWARD DOUBLE DATES

WE HAD MIGRATED to the couch where we were now sitting on opposite ends, pillows in our laps, Taco Bell containers open on the coffee table between us. Ava had wiped away most of the makeup from her face, leaving it blotchy and red. I hadn't bothered with mine, but I'm sure I looked just as cute.

"How long have you known?" was the first question I could think to ask.

She bit her lip and pushed some of her now messy curls out of her face.

"I don't know. I'm not sure I know even now. It was just this nagging suspicion I've had. When Klare seemed a little flirty with me I just... I rolled with it."

"How come you never told me you were... I don't know... suspecting it, I guess?"

She shrugged.

"I don't know. It's not like I was afraid of what you might think. I know you too well for that. Maybe I was just afraid that I didn't want to put it out there if it ended up being nothing."

"I guess I can understand that."

I scooped up the rest of the nacho cheese with a big chip and then set the container aside.

"I'm really sorry I didn't tell you, Ella. I promise. It was never my intention to keep this a secret. I had planned things... differently."

"Hey, don't worry about it. I'm sorry I got all weird about it and stuff. I was just surprised and hurt, but then I realized that I was being selfish. This isn't about me."

"You had a reason to feel hurt, though."

I shrugged.

"It's a thing in the past. Now I want to know the details. This thing between you and Klare, is it legit?"

Ava set her taco wrapper on the coffee table and curled up with her pillow.

"I'm not sure," she answered.

"Would you like it to be?"

For the first time in the last few hours, a smile broke out onto her face.

"Yeah. Yeah, I think I would like that."

"Good! Then you go get her! But... does this mean you'll be dropping out of the experiment?"

She nodded slowly.

"Klare was already going to. I suppose I shouldn't lead Nate on anymore either. It wouldn't be fair to him."

At this, I laughed. Go figure. Ava's the whole reason I was even a part of this whole thing and she's the one that ended up having to drop out.

"You're right," I agreed. "I just hope they take it well, but I'm even more glad things may work out with you and Klare. I mean, look at it this way. The Dating Experiment did technically work out for you, just not the way everyone thought it would."

She smiled.

"That is true."

"Plus!" I added, "Klare is definitely not like all of your past boyfriends. That's for sure. Maybe this is what you were looking for. Maybe this is why none of those guys were working out before."

"That was part of the suspicion," she admitted.

I crawled over and gave her a big hug.

"Are we cool now?" I asked.

She nodded.

"Definitely. Thank you for being so understanding about all of this, especially after the way it all came about. I don't think I can apologize to you enough for springing this on you when you brought August home. Total mood killer!"

I shook it off. It was nothing, really. It's not like I brought him home to have sex. We were definitely not there yet. Yet? Hmm... I suppose I couldn't say for sure whether or not we ever would be. Did I want to have sex with August? I wasn't sure yet. I know it's all stupid and cliche now, to want to save yourself for the right man, but I did want things to be at least a little bit special, and that meant making sure August was the right guy.

"We have more dates to go on," I assured her. "Don't even worry about it."

She sighed and then leaned back to ruffle my hair.

"Hey!"

"I love you, Ella. you're the best little sister I could have asked for."

I fixed my hair, fighting back the sappy little tears that were stinging my eyes.

"I love you too, Sis."

"I'll see you tomorrow alright? I'm pretty beat."

I nodded.

"It's getting pretty late. I think I'm going to go to bed too."

"Good night."

"Good night, Ava."

Ava went straight to bed while I cleared our plates and

crammed the leftover tacos in what little space remained in our refrigerator. Then I checked Cinnabun's water, gave her a late snack, and got ready for bed. I didn't end up getting a lot of sleep that night, but that was alright. I knew I just needed time to let everything sink in, and then everything would be back to normal between me and Ava.

-

I awoke the next morning to a text from August.

August: Good morning! I hope all is well with you and your sister.

Me: Thanks. Things are much better now. We talked. :)

August: I'm really glad to hear that. :)

Me: Our date for today is going to be *here*, if that's alright. It's gonna be a little group thing.

August: Sounds fun!

Me: Good. Come here for 4:00 p.m.

I ran to the grocery store around noon to pick up everything we would need for tonight. Ava, not wanting to be the third wheel, asked if she could invite Klare. Of course I let her. I just hoped Klare wasn't too afraid to come back. I had been so rude to her the night before.

"She'll get over it," Ava assured me. "She's pretty tough."

And I didn't doubt Ava one bit. Klare looked like the kind of woman you didn't want to mess with. She was sweet, but she had this hard edge about her that I couldn't quite put my finger on. That, and she could've beaten me up if she'd wanted to. Easily. One look at all of her toned muscles and I understood that.

Ava helped me put away the groceries when I got home. I showed her the present I found for August when I was out, and she agreed that he was going to love it. She obviously didn't know him as well as I did, but she said he'd be stupid not to.

When the groceries were put away I got dressed in a more "date-like" outfit. Although, if you asked Ava, it was basically just casual attire for me.

"This is literally no different from the outfits you wear every other day," she argued. "It's still got that 1950's housewife trying to fit in with modern society feel going on."

"What is that even supposed to mean?" I'd asked.

"I don't know, but somehow it fits when I look at you."

I did have a thing for high-waisted, tea length skirts and cardigans, but I wouldn't have related my look back to the 1950's... well... until she pointed it out. Then I kind of saw it.

Klare came over just before 3:00 P.M. Her ponytail was, as always, high on her head and sleek. Instead of sports attire, though, she was wearing a pair of jeans and a sweatshirt. It was probably the most relaxed I'd seen her yet. Maybe she understood the night before was just me being shocked. Maybe there would be no need for any awkward tension between us.

"Hi," I said quietly when she sat down on the couch, (at the other end, I might add.) Ava was in the bathroom. "I see you remembered to bring your head."

"Why do your sister and I still need to wear these?"

"Um... well... my sister looks like me, and I don't want August to be getting any clues as to what I look like underneath this panda head," I explained, slapping the panda head perched next to me on the couch. "Ava asked you to bring yours so you wouldn't feel like the odd one out not having one anymore."

She nodded.

"Makes sense. I was just kind of hoping to be done with this damn thing." She lightly kicked the skunk head on the floor."

"One more night," I said. "I promise."

A WHOLE LOT OF PIZZA TOPPINGS

RIGHT AS 4:00 rolled around, so did August.

"If we all know what we're doing," I said to everyone, "We will have these done and ready to eat at 5:30."

"All of us?" Ava questioned.

"Uh. Yeah. What else did you think?"

"That you and August would make them and me and Klare could just eat them."

"Yeah, sadly, that's not how this works. Now suit up. I got us all really cute aprons for this."

August picked one up, flipped it over and laughed.

"They see me rollin'. Ha."

"Alright, so we're going to be making homemade pizzas if you haven't already figured that out from looking at the ingredients in front of you. I figured we could do this in pairs. August and I will make one for ourselves, Ava, you and Klare can make one to share."

"Sounds good to me," Klare agreed.

"Good! Let's get to making this pizza then."

I came prepared. We had all the kinds of cheese and toppings we could ask for. Personally, I preferred to stick to my classic pepperoni and sausage, but Ava and Klare seemed to be getting a little more experimental with theirs.

Admittedly, this was the first time I had realized that making pizza dough is its own unique experience, and is not as simple as mix ingredients and stick in the oven. My baking expertise seemed of no help to me. Luckily, however, August was a much better cooker than he was a baker, so I let him take over for the most part.

"You know they make the dough for you, and you can just bake that and add your own toppings," August pointed out.

I shrugged.

"That is cheating," I argued. "Not truly homemade."

As we made the pizzas, I let Cinnabun out of her cage to run around a bit. (With supervision still, of course.) She seemed to take a liking to August, who absolutely adored her. Ah yes, the key to winning my heart was secretly to gain the affections of my rabbit. Looks like he passed the test.

"How come you never bring Luna with you?" I asked, thinking it would be worth it to see if our pets got along with each other.

He laughed.

"Trust me. You want me to keep her at home for this. I haven't fully trained her that counters and what they hold are off limits. We'd be spending the whole night chasing her away from our food."

"That does make sense. Maybe one of these days you can bring her out on a walk? I'd love to meet her."

"Sure! I believe my sitter wouldn't mind the break either. Poor girl's been watching her a lot lately. I feel sort of guilty. Not just for her, but also for Luna. I know she misses me when I'm gone so much."

"Well, we're more than halfway through this month now, so soon enough you'll be less busy. You can spend all your free time with her. She'll love that."

"Is that to suggest I won't be spending it with anyone else?"

"Oh no! I didn't mean that. I just meant that if you wanted to blow me off for like, a week or so to spend time with your puppy, I'd be okay with that. I think Cinnabun needs some 'me' time as well."

August and I finished first, so we got to put ours in the oven first as well. Once it was cooking, we headed into the living room and I turned on Netflix so we could watch a movie while we waited. This also gave me the perfect opportunity to cuddle into his side with one of his arms wrapped around me. It had been so long since my ex. I'd forgotten what that felt like.

To make things even better, he was absent-mindedly running his fingers along my upper arm, giving me goosebumps. I was smiling underneath my panda mask like a love-struck little school girl. There were so many things I was glad he couldn't see. I mean, I'd known this man for a little over half a month. Was I really this starved for male contact?

"Hey."

He'd leaned down a little to sort of whisper closer to where I'd be able to hear him through the vent in my mask.

"Huh?"

"I know I sort of already asked, but how did things go? I'm assuming well, considering..."

We glanced back toward the kitchen where Ava and Klare were currently hunched over in front of the stove, goading our pizza to cook a little faster so they could put theirs in.

"Yeah. We're all cool now. I really appreciate your concern."

"Of course." He rested his koala head against my panda head. "I care about you."

Queue the butterflies!

(Then also queue the worry, because my brain couldn't let me have this happy moment without at least one "but what if..." Ugh.)

I had to ask.

"Hey, August?"

"Yeah?"

"How, um... how do you feel about, you know, this whole thing between us?"

"What do you mean?"

"I mean... are we just really good friends, or do you see this going elsewhere? I mean, it just feels like... like there's something, I don't know, missing?"

He was quiet for a while, and I wondered if I had just asked a really stupid question, but when he spoke again his answer surprised me.

"Sometimes people fall in love with friends they've had for a long time. Sometimes you develop a love for someone so strong that they also become your best friend. My honest opinion is that even at the end of this, if we're more friends than lovers, that doesn't mean it could never go farther than that."

"That's... kind of a perfect answer."

"DONE!"

August and I both jumped. Ava was standing in the

kitchen with her arms up in the air while Klare took our pizza out of the oven and replaced it with theirs.

"Thanks for that near heart attack, Sis," I complained.

"I'm sorry. I'm just sooo hungry."

I was too. Now that I could smell the pizza in all its warm, cheesy, pepperoni covered glory, my stomach began to rumble like a snow plow barreling through a blizzard. (If you don't happen to have experience with snow and/or plows, it is seriously loud enough to keep people up at night.)

August and I did a good job. Our crust actually raised a little, which I was honestly surprised by, and nothing looked burnt. Now all that was left was a taste test. Unfortunately, the pizza was a little too hot to eat without burning our mouths, (having just gotten out of the oven and all,) so I grabbed us two sodas and we took our dinner back to the couch to continue watching the movie while we waited for it to cool off a little.

When Ava and Klare finally joined us, Ava sat next to me and Klare grabbed the other end. We were a tad smooshed together, but no one seemed to mind much. I sure didn't.

"What did you guys even put on that?" I couldn't help but ask.

Ava thought for a second.

"Umm... chicken, bacon, ranch dressing, mozzarella

cheese, onions, a little bit of parmesan."

"That actually doesn't sound bad at all," August commented.

I agreed.

"I may have to try a piece."

"Not if I eat it all first!" Klare quickly called out.

We all laughed. I didn't know what her fitness routine was, but I will admit that that girl could really put away her pizza for someone so skinny. I *was* literally going to have to race her to the counter if I wanted to get a slice before it was gone.

Meanwhile, I had built up what my sister and I like to refer to as a permanent "food baby." Basically, I have a little bit of a pouch that makes me look somewhere in between I've-put-on-a-little-weight and I'm-in-the-very-early-stages-of-pregnancy. I definitely could not shovel in enough food for three people and still look like Klare, but somehow she managed.

Overall, this date went well. It was nice including my sister for once. Her and August seemed to get along just fine, which you know is always a major worry when you bring a boy home to meet your family.

He very much liked the "Veterinary medicine: Because people are gross" mug that I got him. And, as an added bonus, because of how the other night had gone, I gave him his three questions even though we had ended early. Thankfully, he didn't ask anything too strange, because, you know, my sister was *right there*.

YOU'RE THE MAN

I DON'T KNOW when I fell asleep, but I woke up still on the couch. All the lights were off. The TV was off. Both Ava and Klare were both gone, but August was still beside me, an arm slung around the middle of my body. Somebody had taken the time to cover us up and put Cinnabun to bed.

I tried to get up as quietly and softly as possible, but August still startled awake. His sleepy koala head wobbled a little before he seemed to remember where the extra weight was coming from. He lifted his hands and felt the koala's face.

"What... what time is it?" he asked.

"I don't know. Pretty late, though."

"I should go home."

"Nonsense. Stay here. You can sleep on the couch. I'll leave a note for Ava that you're still here, and I won't come out in the morning until I know your koala head is back in place."

He considered it for a moment, then slowly nodded.

"Yeah. Okay. That sounds good to me. I don't think I'd

make it all the way home."

I smiled to myself.

"Good night, August. I'll see you in the morning."

"Good night."

True to my word, I wrote a note on a stray piece of mail I'd found on the table by the front door and taped it to Ava's bedroom door on the inside, warning her that August was sleeping on the couch. Then I got him another blanket and a pillow and retreated to my own bedroom.

Not that I honestly felt I had to, but just in case, I locked my door once inside. I wasn't afraid of him, or that he might try and cheat. It was just an ease of mind kind of thing, I guess. Either way, I didn't get a whole lot of sleep that night. All I could think about was him curled up on our couch, on the other side of my bedroom door, only so many feet away. Unmasked.

-

The next time I woke up it was light outside, but somehow I knew it was still too early. I was overwhelmed with that groggy sense of not being entirely sure what day it actually was. Then I remembered that there was a semi-strange man sleeping on our couch out in the living room, and so I hastened to get dressed and put my panda head back on.

Before I left my bedroom, I cracked the door open and

called out:

"You up yet?"

"Yeah," came a low, sleepy voice. "You can come out. It's safe."

I tiptoed out of my room, unsure about why I was still being careful. August was wrapped up in the blanket I gave him, a book propped open in his lap.

"Have you been awake long?" I asked.

"No. I only made it through one chapter before I heard you get up."

"Are you hungry? Do you want me to make you something?"

"No. Don't worry about it. I'm just gonna grab a quick coffee and a muffin on my way into work."

"I thought most vet offices were closed on the weekends."

"Sadly, not when you've had to arrange special time off to accommodate your new dating life. I agreed to schedule some appointments for this weekend to make up some of my hours. There are other doctors there to handle things just fine, but some of my patient's owners will only bring their pets to me."

"You must be pretty good, then."

"I like to think so. I put a lot of myself into what I do. It's important to me."

"Well, then I better not keep you too long."

He got up and put the book back in its place on the shelf, then came over to me and gave me a warm hug.

"I'll see you tonight for our date, alright?"

I smiled.

"I'll see you then. Again."

Once he was out the door I stumbled into the kitchen. The digital clock on the stove told me it was only quarter to five in the morning. For the love of God, *why* was I awake? I walked back into the living room and plopped down on the couch. It was still warm where he had been half lying down, so I grabbed the blanket he'd been using and curled up in that spot. It still smelled like warm spices and earthy wood.

-

I called Katie over later on in the day. She'd given me her phone number after that train wreck of a dance class, and I was finally ready to invite her over for another hardcore session. We'd be practicing for hours, or until we passed out from sheer exhaustion, whichever came first.

She arrived about five hours later. Her blonde hair was pulled back into two miniature-sized pigtails, and she had on workout clothing. I was still in my pajamas, as I was too lazy to get dressed for the dance and then get dressed again later for my date. (I know. Mildly pathetic.)

"Did you seriously let him see you in those unicorn shorts?"

I did, and now that my brain was actually registering that fact, I mentally slapped myself.

"I'm just praying he was too tired to really notice, you know?"

"Right. So, are you ready to begin? I thought first we'd watch some instructional videos, and then we can try it out ourselves. I really want you to get a feel for the moves before you attempt them again."

"Yeah. That sounds fine by me."

"Great. Can you pull up Youtube on your TV?"

"Yep."

"Even better!"

Ava didn't question it when she walked out of her bedroom and found Katie and I leaning intently toward the TV, eyes glued to pretty dancers in their leotards. I didn't judge *her* for walking out of her bedroom at almost ten with Klare at her side. If Katie noticed, she didn't even care to say hi. That's how focused she was.

Once the viewing portion was over, we cleared the coffee

table out of the way and pushed the couch back a little bit. Katie and I were almost exactly the same height, so it was hard to maneuver around her like I would with a much taller man, like August, but we did our best. In fact, I barely stepped on her feet at all!

We took things slowly. Much more slowly than our French instructor had us moving. I could do this. I could totally do this. Just a few more run-throughs and I would have it down solid.

"Thanks for doing this for me," I said, as Katie did that thing where the guy twirls the woman under his arm.

I had to duck to make it work, but whatever. It worked.

"Not a problem! Like I said, this isn't a competition or anything. I have no reason *not* to help you. Plus, it's fun. I like dancing."

"I can see that. You're very good at it."

"Thank you! I actually took lessons when I was a little girl but, I haven't danced again since I was twelve, hence the brushing up at Friday classes."

"Well I'm glad, because I really needed someone to help me."

She laughed.

"It's not entirely your fault. Madame Adele is exceptionally hard to understand. It's the male dancers really holding up that class if you ask me."

"Even so. I seemed to have been the only one having the biggest problems."

"And now you're much better! If August falls in love with you over your amazing dance skills, though, make sure to give me the credit I deserve."

"Ha!"

She smiled, and then whisked me around the living room some more. By late in the afternoon, I would have fit right in with the rest of the women in Madame Adele's dance class. Maybe I was even a tiny bit better than some.

THE STATISTICS OF LOVE

THAT NIGHT, AUGUST took me to a concert one of our local bands was putting on. They called themselves Satin Underground, and they were a cover band, but also an *amazing* band. They covered artists such as Van Morrison, Eric Clapton, B.B. King, The Beatles, Bob Segar, The Blues Brothers, Elvis, and Johnny Cash. I was impressed.

I don't know why I feared he would take me to some terrible top 40's radio pop group. August didn't seem like the kind of guy who'd be into that. I guess maybe it was because most guys around my age wouldn't listen to the older stuff anymore. That was our parents' big thing.

"Your choice in music is acceptable," I'd told him.

"Just acceptable?"

"I love it, actually. Although, I think it would be better paired with a Bourbon Cherry Coke, don't you?"

He shook his head, but in a way that told me he was smiling underneath the mask.

"Yeah, I'll take the hint. Be right back."

Who needed mosh pits, and laser lights, and tens of thousands of people when you could sit back at a table no more than twenty feet from the stage, sipping your alcoholic beverage of choice? These were my kind of nights out. And, though we did still practically have to yell to hear each other, at least it *was* possible to talk.

It was a nice night. He even convinced me to get out on the dance floor, which was partially okay with me only because it wasn't slow dancing. It was just fun, silly, you-don't-have-to-be-really-good-at-this dancing. There was no watching where my feet went, or holding onto anyone.

-

The next day we went rummage sale-ing for a little while. This was our last date before the official check-in. The past two Mondays had included check-ins as well, but those ones were not necessary to go to. This Monday's was. It was the Monday of our last official full week.

It was weird, you know? It didn't feel like so much time had passed between that very first introduction day and our last full week. And yet, it also felt like I had known August for longer than that amount of time. It seriously screwed with my head to think about it all, to think about what things were going to be like once this month was over.

Ava had asked me if I was afraid of what his reaction would be upon seeing my face at the reveal ball. I told her I wasn't worried, because I was sure that there was enough of something between us to make that part not matter. (I was hardcore bullshitting.)

In all honesty, I *was* afraid, very afraid. Don't get me wrong. It's not that I've ever thought I was downright ugly. I liked my long, wavy, fiery red hair, my round, hazel eyes, and my freckles. I was of average height. I was a good weight for my age and general size. There were plenty of good things about the way that I looked. It was just that... I also knew I wasn't *every*one's type. Nobody really is. So... what if I wasn't August's?

Even worse. What if he wasn't mine? Would that matter? I could stand up to anyone and say that it absolutely would not, but... that wasn't necessarily true. There was a very real possibility that looks *would* matter in the long run, no matter how badly I wanted them not to.

What if his eyes were too far apart? What if he had a Nanny McPhee level mole, or *two*? What if his teeth were all yellow and he had a unibrow? Would these things make me change my mind about continuing to date him? I honestly couldn't say, and I hated that.

At least our date Sunday had gone well, temporarily distracting me from my maybe-somewhat-shallow thoughts.

-

I still thought about these things, even more, when I walked back into the Center on Monday. Interestingly enough, I was without Ava this time, which should have freaked me out, but somehow didn't. I could sit with Katie. I wasn't alone. August would be there too. This was one of those times where we would all be in the same room.

"How do you think the guys took it?" Katie asked once we were seated. "I mean, they lost their dates when your sister and Klare got together."

There was no secret keeping. I had to tell Katie why both Klare and Ava hadn't shown up. I figured she was going to find out anyway, even though she had somehow missed the previously mentioned early morning scenario. Maybe I should give her credit, though. It wasn't too unlikely for grown women to simply have a casual sleepover... was it?

I shrugged.

"I'm sure they were disappointed, but I don't think there's anything they could have done about it."

"Yeah... probably not."

"Good Morning!" Holly Van Warden stepped up to her

podium and smiled that perfectly white smile of hers. "How are you all doing today?" There were mumbled answers all around the room. "As you all know," she continued, seemingly ignoring whatever anyone actually said, "This is the last official full week of the Dating Experiment!

"The Reveal Ball is just around the corner, meaning you should hurry on up and get ahold of your attire for the evening before it's too late to get fitted and have alterations if needed. Remember, we expect you to dress your best. The event will be held on the second floor of this building, in a room specially designed for this occasion, and it's sure to be a dazzling night for all!"

Queue all of my rude eye rolling that she thankfully couldn't see.

"Anyway," Holly continued. "Today we are here to check in with everyone. It won't take long, but we'd like you each to have a little one-on-one session talking to our statistical geniuses who also happen to be your matchmakers. Rest assured won't be any uncomfortable or difficult questions, we just want to get an idea of how things have been going. This helps us in the long run when we use the information you provide us to better future Experiments."

Huh... it was almost like an exit survey, one that they had

successfully tricked us into. Instead of sending one out after the whole thing was said and done, they were clever enough to make this meeting sound ultra-important so we would show up. Smooth. Real smooth.

"Lame," said Katie.

I agreed. Then we were broken up and sent into different rooms with one of the "statistical geniuses."

"Hello!" the women greeted me as we walked through the door. "Please, have a seat." She gestured to the table, so I took one of the little, plastic chairs across from her. "My name is Amanda, and you are?"

"Ella."

"Ah, yes! Ella Carter. And how do you feel your experience has been going so far?"

"Pretty good. No complaints."

"Good, good. And do you believe we have done a successful job of pairing here at the Dating Experiment Center?"

"Um... yeah. I guess so. The sheep was a little out in left field, but the other two were good."

"Ah, yes. Sometimes that does happen. I'll admit that the Dating Experiment is only as successful as the participants are honest. I'm sorry your first experience didn't please you."

"It's okay. It made my decision that much easier."

"That it did," she replied with a bright smile. "And I see that you picked your second choice, Mr. LaMarche."

"Uh... yeah."

I suppose I did, though this was the first time I remembered that August had to have a last name. I hadn't known what it was before. It never really came up. I never told him mine either. Well, now he would know anyway, so there was that. Out of the way.

"And how do you think things are going, specifically with August?"

I was about to fight a giddy smile when I realized that she wouldn't be able to see it anyway.

"Good. Really good. I mean... great, even. I guess."

"Care to elaborate?"

"Uhh... I mean... we get along really well. He's a nice guy. We have things in common, including values. He's funny. Sweet. Weird, but in a good way. We haven't really lost too many question points even, because we like a lot of the same things and places."

"That's very good to hear! As things stand now, would you like to stay with him long term, then?" I nodded. "Good! I'm glad to hear that. Hearing the success stories of this Experiment are one of my favorite parts of doing this job."

"I can imagine."

"So, one last question."

"Okay..."

"Do you believe your opinion could change on the evening of the Reveal Ball?"

This one I had to think about. Here she was, asking that stupid question that had already been running through my mind. All distraction gone. It was right there in front of my face.

I answered as honestly as I could.

"There's always that chance, isn't there? I believe in my heart, though, that the possibility is very low. I like him a lot. Maybe I'm even falling in love with him. I don't know. I do know, however, that there would have to be an extreme reason for me to walk away from him."

LET'S TIE THIS UP

I WANTED SO badly to ask August what he'd said about me, but there was a reason they made us go into separate rooms. It was just... it was killing me not knowing what he thought of all this. I, on the other hand, practically admitted to falling in love with him. Was I? I didn't even know for sure. Maybe... a little... It's not like I had been in love before to know what that felt like.

In retrospect, I didn't have to wait too long to find out, though. There were two dates. One the afternoon of the check-in, where he took me to get ice cream and gave me a bath bomb set. One where I made him go pottery painting, and gave him a small notepad and a pen. Both of those were fun, light-hearted, easy dates. THEN... he sprung on me THE DATE.

Okay, so it's not like either of us knew exactly how this was going to go walking into it, so maybe I shouldn't say that he sprung it on me. It just happened to be his date. That's all. He'd slept at my apartment on my couch and that wasn't planned. Neither of us considered me springing anything on him *that* time.

But this was so... different. Romantic and special and everything I could have hoped that it would be for a 21st date.

First, he invited me to his apartment for a homemade meal, and his apartment was about ten times better than Ava's. (Not that I didn't love hers.) It was a one bedroom, but the living room and kitchen were much bigger. Plus, he had his own private, gated patio off of the living room. While he was cooking dinner, I sat out on a lounge chair with Luna curled up on the deck at the end of the chair.

She was the sweetest puppy I'd ever seen. Of course, she was also hyper and had a knack for getting into things. Part of why she was out with me was so she wouldn't get into the kitchen while August was cooking. I didn't mind. Once she calmed down she just wanted to lie close to someone and snooze.

For dinner, he was making alfredo stuffed shells. I liked regular chicken and broccoli alfredo, so I didn't see why I wouldn't like it stuffed in shells. Of course, he told me to expect something even better than what I originally imagined, because it was his mom's own recipe and it wasn't like any other. I liked that he was close to his family, especially his mother. I also wondered if one day I would be able to meet them.

The patio door slid open.

"Dinner's almost done," he announced. "Do you want to

eat out here?"

"Yes, please. It's so nice out."

And it really was. The weather was still warm, but not too warm for me to wear a flowing, long-sleeved shirt that swished around my arms.

"Alright. I'll be out in just a minute then. Come on, Luna!"

Luna instinctively hopped up and ran to him, probably unaware that she was going to get put inside. She just liked August. He never had to worry about her not coming when he called, which I thought was totally adorable. I wished Cinnabun would come to me when I called, but I guess that just wasn't how bunnies were, no matter how much they liked you.

August brought out a tray balancing our plates and drinks and set it on the little round table with wicker chairs. I moved over and we sat down across from each other. It was a little later in the day when dinner got done, so the sun was already quite low in the sky.

"This is pretty cliche," I pointed out. "Romantic, homemade dinner on your balcony, setting sun. All we're missing is the candlelight."

He laughed.

"I did think about bringing candles out here, but then I thought about the risk of balancing them and potentially catching my apartment on fire, so... here we are."

"You really did think about it, though?"

He nodded.

"It's not only women who like cliche, romantic dinners. Us hopeless romantic men are into it as well."

I smiled. How could I possibly meet a guy this perfect? There had to be something wrong with him. There just had to be. Right?

We talked while we ate. He later brought out dessert, which was a chocolate lava cake that we had to split, because it was so rich. I mean, I would have eaten the whole thing myself, but then I also probably would have gone into a sugar coma, because man, was that cake chocolate-y or what!

"And you made this?" I'd asked.

He nodded.

"Of course."

"I thought you couldn't bake?"

"Depends what it is. My mother taught me this one."

We sat out on the balcony for a little while longer, talking about anything and everything, then we retreated back inside. I plopped on the couch with him. At this time, Luna was tucked away in his bedroom, so there were no distractions. Just me and him. On his couch. Him leaning over the side to pull a bag out that he had been hiding.

"My present?"

"Duh!" I flung my hands out and excitedly grabbed at the pink, sparkly bag. "Hey now," he said. "Have a little patience."

He laughed and handed me the bag. Ignoring that comment, I dug in and ripped out all of the tissue paper to reveal a fuzzy, lumpy thing at the bottom of the bag. I pulled it out. It was a sandy colored, stuffed, lop-eared bunny. I looked just like Cinnabun.

"Oh my, God! I love this!" I hugged the stuffed bunny to me. "Thank you so much! It looks just like her."

He had turned to face me, but other than that, I had no idea what his reaction was. I wished, for the millionth time, that I could see the smile that just had to be on his face.

"I saw it and knew I had to get it for you that instant."

"It's perfect. If I could kiss you right now, I so would. This date has been perfect."

"So why don't you?"

I paused, watching him. He was so still that I imagined the look on his face must have been a serious one. But... how could he be serious? Kissing him meant taking the heads off, and we weren't supposed to do that yet.

"Uh... I... We can't...," I finally choked out.

"We can make it work. We can... do it in a dark room, or find a way to cover our eyes."

My heartbeat sped up.

"You're serious."

"Yes. Very."

"You really want to kiss me?"

He reached forward and took both my hands in his. Our stupid animal faces were only inches apart.

"Yes. I do."

I couldn't fight my smile.

"I do too. Let's do this! What do you have that could work as a blindfold?"

We brainstormed together.

T-shirts. (Too large.) Toilet paper. (Too weird. Prone to rip.) A hat. (Might slip up.) Duct tape. (Desperate much? Too painful to take off.) His work ties...

"Ties!" we both agreed in unison.

(God, what had my life come to?)

"I'll go grab two."

He disappeared into his bedroom and I sat on the couch, giddy with the thought of finally being able to kiss August, even if we had to be a little unconventional about how we made it happen. Was it weird? Yes. Did it seem a little too far on the kinky side? Yes. But at the time, that's just how it had to be. All we wanted to do was finally share our first kiss.

He came back and handed me a soft, blue, plaid tie. I went into the bathroom to put it on while he stayed outside the door so we wouldn't be too far apart and have to stumble around the place looking for one another. He may have been familiar enough with his apartment, but I was bound to trip and knock over every damn thing that was unfortunate enough to end up in my way.

Once my tie was secure, and I doubled it up just to be sure, I turned the light off and opened the door.

"You good?" I asked.

"Yep. Right here."

I felt around the space before me and eventually hit the hand that he was holding out. He pulled me to him until we were standing so close that my chest was pressed up against his.

"So... that kiss," I said, being awkward in that way that I've always been good at.

He put his hands on my waist. I moved mine up his arms, to his shoulders, his neck, and finally his cheeks, which were covered in a short layer of stubble. My heart wasn't necessarily racing at this point, but it was thumping so hard in my chest that I was sure even he could feel it.

I took a moment to caress his face, taking in his strong cheekbones and angled jawline before pushing up onto my tippy toes and running my thumb over his lips to make sure I planted my kiss in the right spot.

They were soft and warm, and when I kissed him his stubble brushed up against my cheek and I loved the feeling of it. Up close like this, I was drowning in that spicy, earthy scent of his, and I didn't want to save myself. I didn't need air. I had August. And that's all I needed in that moment.

FEELING IS BELIEVING

I THOUGH THAT was where things would end, but... I was definitely wrong. And I'm not saying that like it's a bad thing, because it was most certainly not a bad thing. Am I going to lie and say that losing my virginity blindfolded wasn't a weird thing? No. But, it was better than "getting it over with via a drunken one-night-stand," which is what Ava had started suggesting about a year prior. So... there *was* that.

Plus, it was super amazing. August was a complete gentleman about it, because I had admitted to him once things began to get a little more heated that this wasn't something I'd ever done before, and not just the blindfolded part. I told him that it was just something that never happened for me and he was understanding. It didn't bother him, thankfully.

As we kissed, I ran my hands up through his soft, curly hair that was longer on top but trimmed short on the sides and in the back. I felt his ears, his nose, his face change when he smiled. And then I buried my face in the crook of his neck as he ran his hands through my long curls I had let down.

I couldn't get enough of this man I didn't fully know yet. Somehow,I just knew, as unconventional as the situation was, I was making the right choice.

"W-would it be weird if... we...?"

I just didn't want to be the one to suggest it, because, you know, the situation and all. I didn't know at the time if he was going to be into or not. (And I already know what you're thinking. He's a man! Of course! But not all guys are the same, okay?)

"If we..."

Oh, God. He didn't get it. Great.

"Um... you know, took this farther?"

"Oh! Well... um... I don't... I don't necessarily think so. Different, but not too weird... maybe."

"I just... I feel like I know you well enough and, well, I want to."

I really did. Screw it. I needed to get laid already. August seemed like a good enough guy, so what more did I really need?

"Okay then. I can't say I disagree with you there."

He led me with one hand and felt for the bedroom door with the other. We shooed Luna out of the room when she happily came to greet us. August proceeded to run into his bed, almost toppling us both over when it caused him to lose his balance.

"Oh my, God!" I exclaimed. "Are we fucking crazy?"

He laughed.

"Maybe a little. But who says crazy can't be good?"

I can't lie, the whole situation was sort of funny, and we couldn't stop laughing. It eased any tension I may have had, caused me to relax. It didn't feel too serious, just kind of silly. (Okay. *Really* silly.) My heart stopped feeling like thunder in my chest. I was able to lie down next to him and feel more at ease than I had been expecting.

"Are you sure this is how you want it to happen?" he'd asked after my admission of virginity.

I nodded.

"I like you. I'm not getting any younger. Plus, I'm not some naive teenager. I'm good."

"I just want to make sure."

I smiled.

"And that's how I know I'm making the right call."

Now, I'm not gonna go into all the unnecessary details of what transpired, because I'm pretty sure that's obvious. I will say one thing, though. It was nice because nothing was rushed. He understood that I needed to take things slower and, honestly, we sort of had to whether we wanted to or not. There needed to be a lot of feeling around to make sure we didn't jab one another in the eye, or try and stick anything where it didn't belong.

Confirmed: One of the weirdest yet best moments of my relatively short life thus far. Maybe it worked out so well because August and I were just a weird kind of people. I don't really know. 10/10 would not take back for anything in the world.

-

If I'm being honest, one of my more favorite parts of that date was waking up in the morning. Aside from sleepovers with friends that I had back in elementary and middle school, this was the first time I had woken up in someone else's home. First time it was a boy's home.   Or, man's, in this case. God, that felt strange to me.

That, and I was wrapped up in a blanket, snuggled up to his side, one arm stretched out across his bare chest. He was still asleep, that much I knew. I couldn't see, but I could hear the way his breathing was different from when he was awake. More even. If I never had to move I wouldn't have, because this was a kind of comfort I had never been able to experience. I wanted to hold onto it.

I shifted just a little bit. Luna must have been right outside the door, because upon doing so, I heard her get up off the floor and start barking at the door. So much for holding onto that moment. August was awake instantly.

"Ah, crap. I have to take her out. I'll, uh... I'll be right back."

He climbed out of bed and did his best to put pants on, though it sounded like a struggle. From there I could hear him stumbling into various other things as he left the room. There was a curse word or two thrown into his cheerful talking-to-puppy voice and, admittedly, it made me giggle. Every. Single. Time. Poor August. I'm sure once he figured out I was still safely in his room he remembered that he could move the mask to see where he was going. (At least I sure *hope* he did.)

Thankfully, after making his way back into the room, more smoothly than he left, he sat down on the edge of the bed and sighed.

"She almost tripped me. Ran right in front of my path. If I hadn't been so cautious you would have had a whole lot more to laugh about."

I cringed.

"You could hear that?"

"These walls aren't very thick, sorry to say."

"My bad. But you have to admit, in my situation, you probably would have been giggling too."

"Oh, most definitely."

"So..."

"So?" he questioned.

"I should probably get dressed, huh?" I responded. "As nice as it would be to stay in here with you, I signed up for an early shift and I only have... uh... what time is it?"

"Quarter after four."

"Ugh. I only have forty-five minutes!"

"I suppose you should then. I'll help you to the bathroom."

I climbed out of bed and tried to grab what I assumed to be my own clothing off the floor. August held his hand out for me, which I aimlessly groped around for, and then stood up. He got the door open, but then I heard a thud and a grunt that told me his judgment had been slightly off.

"Sorry," he said. "Hit the door frame. Watch out."

He felt along the opposite wall once we made it out of the bedroom, searching for the bathroom door. After all of that, we were finally back to our normal selves. Okay, our normal Dating Experiment selves. Animal masks and all.

"Did you see my...?"

I was about to ask if he'd seen my underwear, as that was the only thing I seemed to be missing, when he held them up for me. My face turned beet red, I just knew it. I could feel the burning.

"These, right?"

"Yes. Thank you."

I tried to play it off cool, but honestly, I was dying on the inside. A grown ass man was holding my lacy, little, black panties like it was nothing. I hoped that didn't mean it was something he was used to doing often. Not sure how I'd have felt about that.

"I'm really glad we did this," he admitted. "Not in like, a pervy I'm-just-happy-because-sex kind of way, but like... I really like you, and this was fun. Weird, but fun. And I like you a lot."

(Eek).

"I'm glad too. I also really like you a lot."

I wished I could see if he was smiling, because I sure was.

"Have a good day, Ella. Enjoy work. I look forward to seeing you later today."

"Thanks. You have a good day, too."

I practically skipped down the steps from there.

TIGHT-LIPPED AND SPARKLY

"O.M.G! YOU HAVE to tell me everything!"

I'd stumbled in at 4:30 a.m., only half an hour before my work shift started.

"I'm not telling my sister about losing my virginity."

Ava huffed and smacked me with a pillow.

"If you can't tell your sister, who do you plan to tell?"

"Um... nobody?"

She rolled her eyes.

"Lame."

Whatever. What went on between me and August during our night together was nobody's business but mine as his. Besides... talking about sex made me feel uncomfortable. It's not like I was a prude or anything, it's just, you know, some people are more open about that kind of stuff. I wasn't one of those people. I had nothing against sex. I just didn't want to discuss the details of it with people other than the one I was having the sex with.

Also, there were other matters we had to attend to.

"Hey, you're still going to the Reveal Ball, right?" I asked.

Ava plopped down onto my bed, looking a little disappointed.

"Why would I? I dropped out."

"Not really. You did meet someone, and it *was* because of the Dating Experiment. I think you two should go. Have a grand reveal of your own, if that's something you're comfortable with at this stage."

"Oh, you know me. I'd love to make a grand entrance into homosexuality by revealing the secret at the Reveal Ball. I'm just... I'm not sure."

"It'll be fine. Plus, I'd really like to have my sister there. You got me into this whole thing, after all."

"Yeah, and look how that turned out. You got your dream man, which is what I'd been hoping for in the beginning. I found out I like women and dropped out. Funny, huh?"

"A bit, actually, but that doesn't mean you can't go. You did pay for all of this. They can't stop you. Come on!" I tried to appeal to her through her love of shopping and fashion. "You have to at least go dress shopping with me. If we happen to find something for you, you're going." (It was a trap. I *knew* she would most likely end up finding something.)

She smiled and got that excited look about her that told me she couldn't resist.

"Okay fine! You got me!"

-

I took the early work shift so I could be off by noon that day. Once I returned home, Ava and I hit this cute little boutique called Azalea Park. I even told her she could invite Klare, who joined us down at the store after getting back from her morning jog. To my surprise, she seemed super excited about the idea of doing their own special reveal at the ball.

"Alright, I'm looking for simple, but still stunning," I said. "Nothing too over the top."

"I want all of the sparkles!" Ava called out.

Klare smiled mischievously.

"I know this may be a little stereotypical, but since I'm tall enough to pull it off, I want to be wearing a suit. You know, play with people a little bit."

Ava laughed.

"Genius! We must find Klare a suit when we're done."

The lady helping us pulled several dresses off the rack for both me and Ava, enough that we each had a pile forming in our dressing rooms. Mine were pretty, but a little laid back. Ava's had all the glitz and glam she was looking for. Klare, with all of the patience in the world, sat out on a bench giving us feedback as we stepped out to show her each dress.

My first one was a soft blush pink and, although it looked great with my hair and my skin, I felt like it was a little too subdued. I did like that it was flowing at the bottom, though. It felt nice when I moved and did that princess twirl where I spun around like they always do in the movies.

The second dress I tried on was olive green. It brought out the hints of green in my hazel eyes, but other than that I thought it made my head look like a pumpkin overwhelmed by its vines, because of my bright, orange-ish red hair and all.

Numbers three and four were immediate no-gos, because the woman helping us had wanted to try something a little more experimental, but I wasn't a fan of the half-naked feel of the skin-tone lace. Sure, everything that needed to be covered up was, but I felt like one slip would send the whole night into an embarrassment for me real fast.

The fifth one was perfect. It was a deep garnet red dress with an off the shoulder, sweetheart neckline. The bottom was fitted to my curves, but not too tightly, and it flowed out at the bottom. It looked stunning with my red hair, just as I hoped it would. I spun around in the mirror, examining myself from all angles.

"It's perfect for you, Ella," said Klare. "You look very grown up in it."

I felt grown up. I felt like a powerful career woman who didn't put up with anyone's shit. Was I? Not in the slightest, but it was sure nice to feel like it in that dress. I smiled and turned to the boutique woman, whose name I eventually learned was Karen.

"I will take this one!"

It took another half hour to find one suitable for Ava and, in the end, she finally decided on a strapless, sweetheart neckline dress in navy blue that was covered in sequins from top to bottom. It flowed out from the silky band at her waist and swished like water when she moved. Very Ava-esque.

Klare's face lit up when Ava walked out of the dressing room stall.

"You look absolutely gorgeous," she said, standing to take a closer looked.

Ava spun on the spot.

"I feel absolutely gorgeous!"

"And will this be the one for you then?" Karen asked. "You do look very beautiful in it."

"Thank you. This will definitely be the one."

Thankfully, as we were doing this a tad bit late, there

weren't many alterations that needed to be done. Mostly, it was only length that needed to be taken off. Karen took our measurements and told us she would have someone get to it right away. We were scheduled to be back in for a fitting on Monday the 29th.

"I hope that gives us enough time," said Ava. "That's only two days before the ball."

"I'm sure it will be fine," I assured her. "There's not much they have to do."

"Plus," Klare added. "I feel like this is something they have to deal with regularly because of the Dating Experiment. It's not like prom where you have months to plan. She'll more than likely have a whole team of people getting these ready for next Wednesday."

On that note, and I was sure it was a correct one, we headed off to one of the men's tuxedo shops to see if we could convince them to let Klare get fitted for a suit.

Overall, it was a fun day and, after I got back from dress shopping, August came to pick me up for our next date. This time we were going to a cute, little, used bookstore a few blocks away. Personally, I had been there probably a hundred times since I moved in with Ava. It was something I wanted to share with August, because it was one of my favorite places in the city.

Remembering the night before made my cheeks blush just thinking about him coming over, and Ava got on my case about it relentlessly. Eventually, she even spilled the news to Klare, and I wanted to bury my head in a hole for the rest of my life. So August and I had sex. What was the big deal?

Other than the fact that those were words I'd never been able to use before in my twenty-six years.

LET'S BE DIRTY TOGETHER

AUGUST AND I were alone again for the first time since we'd slept together... literally hours ago. Somehow, this brought out all of the awkwardness I could afford to share. I mean, we'd been so comfortable together, obviously, right up until this one moment. Why would I be nervous? It was something I had wanted to do. It was romantic. It wasn't bad or, like, scary or anything. I enjoyed that night, even after I'd left. So what was wrong with me now?

I didn't want to be weird about it. I didn't want him to think it was a mistake, that I regretted any part of it. Because I didn't. I really didn't. It wasn't a question in my mind. It was a fact.

We were at me and Ava's apartment that night, playing Scrabble at the coffee table. (I know, two dates in one day was technically cheating, but we just hadn't wanted to end yet.) Honestly, it was more like one long, extended date.

So far, he was in the lead by a whopping seventy points. I liked to think it was because I was distracted, but I couldn't deny the fact that August was also simply good at Scrabble. For the most part, we were quiet.

"Everything okay?" he finally asked.

I looked up from where I had been staring at my row of letters.

"Yeah... everything's fine."

"You're particularly quiet."

"I'm just... concentrating. That's all. I'm trying to figure out how I can turn this game around so I can still kick your butt."

He laughed softly, but there was still an unsureness about it. I don't think I was fooling either one of us.

Cinnabun was in her cage, napping in a corner. Luna was on a leash that August had wrapped around the couch so she could only go so far. Currently, her nose was pressed up against the side of Cinnabun's cage, and that was her limit. They had sniffed each other out a bit, but otherwise Cinnabun didn't seem to care about Luna's presence.

"Do you think this is going to work?" I asked, mainly to change the subject.

I nodded my panda head toward our pets. August followed my gaze and watched them a little bit. Luna was pretending to be asleep, but every time Cinnabun so much as twitched, Luna's head snapped up and she sniffed around again.

"I sure hope so. Otherwise, we're going to have to think

up some kind of arranged living situation for them where they're not in the same place at the same time. I know Luna probably just wants to play, but she might be a little too rough with Cinnabun, and we wouldn't want that. Luna could easily hurt her without meaning to."

I played "mines" for fourteen points. Stupid bad letters.

"I'd really hate to have to leave you because our pets can't live together," I joked.

"And that would be the only reason?"

My brows furrowed.

"What do you mean?"

He let out a long sigh.

"I'm sorry. I didn't mean it to come out like an accusation or anything. It just..." He was quiet a moment. "It just feels like something's... different... between us. You've been quiet tonight, and you keep staring at those game pieces like they're going to jump off the table if you're *not* looking."

Ah crap.

"Everything is fine, August. I'm fine. Stop worrying about it."

He sat back, and I got the immediate feeling that I had said something wrong.

"I can't help but worry a little, Ella. Women I've had sex

with don't usually have a problem so much as looking in my direction afterward. I kind of feel like that might mean something in this case."

Ah, continued crap.

"Well, maybe you're just reading into things a little too much," I spat out, which, in retrospect, I wanted to take back immediately.

Stupid mouth.

He sighed again, staring me down. I wanted to curl my whole body up into the panda head to get away from the glare I knew his eyes were holding on me.

"So, what? I'm just imagining things? You're telling me that absolutely nothing is going on here, and that I must be crazy, because all I can see is a woman who looks uncomfortable being around me?"

"I'm not uncomfortable being around you. I swear. It's... It's not that."

"But it is *some*thing..."

And then I knew. I had my answer. The answer to the question the Center woman, Amanda, had asked. I could never change my mind. Not now.

"I'm scared, August." My eyes welled up under my mask. I was thankful he couldn't see. Not that I believed he couldn't hear it in my voice anyway. "I'm scared that... even though I now know that I wouldn't change my mind about you in the end... maybe you'll change yours."

"Ella," he whispered, his voice so soft.

"I don't know what it's like to fall in love with someone," I continued, stopping him from going on. "I've never done that before, and... well... I'm still pretty sure that I might be falling in love with you. Yesterday night meant so much to me. You know that. You've slept with other woman, but you were my first, and I don't want to sound like one of those clingy girls who fall for the first person they have sex with, because it's not about that. I was already falling for you before then. I wouldn't have gone through with it otherwise..."

"Ella, please..." he interrupted again, but I was on a roll.

"I don't know if I just sound pathetic now, or what, but what I do know is that there is a very real chance that come next Wednesday you will decide you don't want me and I'll have to live with that and... and I don't want to have to..."

"Ella!" This time I stopped. He never raised his voice at me like that before. "Please, just... breathe."

I took a deep breath and let it out slowly through pursed lips.

"I'm sorry," I mumbled

"Don't be." He moved around the table and came to my side, putting an arm around my shoulder and pulling me to him. "I'm sorry too. I was pushing you."

"But you were right."

"Still. I just... I don't want you to think like that, Ella. I don't want you to think that I'm just going to walk away at the end of all of this. That night, as... *different* as it was, meant something to me too. I like you. A lot. Maybe I'm falling in love with you too... I don't know. It seems weird to think that we could fall in love without really getting to know each other the way people normally do.

"I'd love to actually get to know your sister and hear adorable stories she has from when you were growing up together. I'd like to see cute photos of you that you'd find embarrassing. I want to see you do the things you're passionate about, like your work. There are so many things we don't know about each other, but... I honestly feel like I *couldn't* just walk away at the end of all of this."

God, he was so sweet, even after I was sort of rude about the whole thing. I leaned and rested my panda head against his chest. He wrapped both arms around me and squeezed tight.

"I understand perfectly what you mean," I said after a small bit of silence. "There are things I'd like to do and see as well.

I know you have a family." I laughed. "Unless you're an alien who was dropped on Earth all by yourself, but I bet you're not. I'd like to meet them someday. I'd like to know what you're like when you're not trying to impress me."

"You want me to show up on our next date in my pajamas? I can skip getting ready in the morning. I'll get you an orange or something else that I dug out of my fridge, and we can spend our time together doing my laundry. I'll even let you fold."

I cracked a big smile, giggling like a little school girl.

"I would like that very much."

He laughed too.

"It's a deal, but only if you come in pajamas as well. With oversized, rumpled up socks. Ooh! And don't bathe or anything. We'll just bask in each other's filth the whole time."

"Oh, my God!" I playfully slapped him, but we both continued to laugh. "You are terrible."

Kelli Rajala

PASS-TEES, NOT PAY-STEES

IT WAS GOOD that I'd opened up to August. A sense of relief washed over me that day, especially when he confirmed that he really liked me too, and that it would be unlikely anything could make him walk away. We were on the same page. That was good.

In fact, we spent most of the weekend together, and none of it was awkward anymore. We were just two people who really liked each other, having fun going thrift shopping and trying on all the weird clothes we found. We ate fast food for dinner and asked each other trivial questions for the first time, such as;

"What's your favorite color?"

Everyone's number one go-to. My answer was aqua, in case you were wondering.

"What one food do you absolutely hate?"

His answer was pasties. (Pronounced pass-tees.) *Not pay-stees, those things you put on your boobs to cover up the nipple.* That aside, this is also how I learned he was from Northern Michigan. Apparently, pasties are a big thing there, and he's always been the odd duck out for thinking they were gross. Understandable. When someone says pastry, I want a dessert, not meat and potatoes and other things stuffed into a crust. Gross.

"What's your favorite TV show?"

Uh. Easy! Literally any baking competition show. He probably should have known that answer by now. If I had to pick *one*, though, I'd probably say Cupcake Wars.

"What's your favorite season?"

He picked fall, and no, it had nothing to do with his name. It had more to do with sweater weather, coffee, leaves changing color, and pumpkin flavored everything. All reasons I was in 100% agreement with. I sometimes hated to admit this, but mostly the pumpkin flavored everything reason. I know. I was one of *those* girls.

"Do you have a suit all picked out for Wednesday?" I asked.

"I do."

"It's not one of those ones we found at Goodwill, is it?"

He laughed.

"No. I promise I got a real one. It's even got the red vest and bow-tie that will match your dress."

I had shown him a sample of the color, because I thought it would be cuter if we were matching. I know. Cheesy.

"Aw! This is going to feel like high school prom all over again. We can relive our youth."

"Except this time I know how to dance a little better, and I'm not going to be hiding out by the food table while my date dances with another guy," he admitted.

"Ouch..."

"Yeah. It was an awkward experience. But the second year I at least learned that if I brought a plastic Walmart bag with me, I could fill it at the end of the night, because they didn't want to waste all of the snacks. They let us take whatever we could carry. Shame I didn't know that the first time around."

I shook my head.

"I'm not sure if that's sad or funny, honestly."

"Maybe a little of both."

"Not a fan of the whole reliving our youth idea, then?"

He shook his head.

"High school was definitely not the highlight of my life, but that's good, right? They say if you peak in high school it's all basically downhill from there."

"You have a good point. You just planned to make sure you didn't peak too early. You wanna be on the upswing longer, enjoy it, bask in it."

"Exactly."

He took my hand in his and gave it a light squeeze.

-

"Are we going to get our hair done professionally?" Ava asked when I got home late Sunday evening.

I shrugged.

"That's up to you, I guess. We're still going to have the heads on, so it'll have to be in an updo either way. I'm not sure I need to pay someone to do that."

"Yeah, but you could get a really cute, *fancy* updo. I mean, please don't tell me you're considering throwing your hair up in a bun like you normally do. The panda head will be coming off, after all."

I sighed. She was right. She also knew me well, because that was exactly what I had been planning. I guess I didn't think that August's opinion of me was going to hinge on how well I could do my own hair. Though I suppose there was no way to know that it wouldn't. Maybe that was his thing. Maybe he had a pristine hair fetish I just didn't know about yet.

"Fine," I caved. "Schedule us appointments soon then. I want to make sure I get Lacey again. I really like what she can do with my hair. It's like she knows it on a personal level."

"First thing when they open tomorrow, I'll give them a call."

She practically bounced back into her room. Ava was still more excited about this whole deal than I was, but I guess that wasn't too surprising. Have I ever mentioned that I seemed to be less capable of showing excitement than most people I knew? No? Well, it was true. My whole life I'd been like that. You could tell me you just bought me tickets to Avril Lavigne (I was obsessed with her when I was little) and I'd be like "Awesome!" No jumping, no screeching, no crying. Just... "Awesome!"

Ava was the exact opposite in that respect.

-

I was so close to seeing August for the first time. I knew details. He had a mop of curls on top of his head, but the sides and back were shaved relatively short. He had a narrow jawline and strong cheekbones. He kept his facial hair trimmed neatly and close to the skin. He had soft lips. He was tall, with long, slender limbs. I didn't have a full picture, though.

What color were his eyes? What color was his hair? Did he have tattoos? What did he look like when he smiled? Did his eyes light up? Did his cheeks flush red? Was his smile as cute as I imagined it would be?

Everything was coming to a head so quickly now. The hours felt like minutes. Seconds, sometimes. Maybe I was simply getting nervous. I don't know. He had reassured me the other night, and I knew how I felt about him, but there was something about only ever knowing somebody without a face. And then... suddenly they have one. Or, they always did, but you couldn't see it, and now you can. It was weird. It felt... weird... to think about.

Sometimes you grow used to things the way they are. That's something I've done my whole life up until the Dating Experiment started. August was just another part of that. Like meeting Katie, going on adventures with strange men I didn't know, and trying new things in new places it was time for me to admit that the masks were coming off. It wouldn't really be fair to August if I told him that in order to date we had to keep them on. That would just be ridiculous.

I pulled my blanket up over my shoulders and wiggled down so that my head was low on my pillow. I was completely submerged in the safe comfort of my fluffy bedding. My room was dimly lit with a small night light plugged in on the opposite wall. Cinnabun could be heard shuffling around in her cage. Everything else was quiet.

Just a few more days. I could do this. Just a few more days, but that was okay. Everything was going to be okay. There was no reason to be afraid. This is what the whole thing had been leading to from the beginning. I knew that. There was *no* reason to be afraid.

WATCH WHERE YOU PUT YOUR HANDS

KATIE WENT WITH us to the dress shop. Hers was already picked out, paid for, and altered, but she wanted to share the experience with us since she had gone alone for her own. I'll admit, it was nice having her there as *my* buddy, since Ava had Klare.

There we two teams of women working on our dresses, so we got to do our fittings at the same time. Currently, there was one lady on the floor, examining the part that had been made shorter and making sure it was even all the way around. Another woman was sticking her hand down the front of my dress. She gave me a sharp look when I flinched at her hand grazing my left breast.

"I'm just checking to make sure the cups of this dress are in their proper place," she informed me in a mildly harsh tone.

Katie snickered across the room. I apologized. I shouldn't have had to, if we're being honest. It's not like I let strange people go sticking their hands all up in my shirt all the time. She could have at least warned me. Or, I don't know, maybe I would have been capable of doing that part myself?

"Looks like you're good up top," said the boob groper. "How is it looking down there, Kathleen?"

"Looks good to me too. Just a few touch-ups needed. Pretty simple."

Once Kathleen was done I went back to the dressing room and got changed into my regular outfit. After I was clothed again, I carried out the shoes I'd borrowed for height and threw away those stupid little nylon socks they make you wear.

"You're going to look so beautiful!" Katie said as I approached her. "You'll be turning heads."

She wasn't wrong about the turning of heads part, but we'll follow up with that later on.

"You're going to look just as pretty," I told her.

She was going to be wearing a pale pink v-neck gown with cap shoulders and beautiful lace detailing. She was going to look like a little princess, and what prince wouldn't want to find his princess and possible future queen?

Ava's fitting was quick too. Once we were done we headed out shoe shopping, which had always been one thing we both loved to do, especially together. Klare and Katie sort of got caught up in all of our craziness as we pro-level fangirled over almost all of the shoes in the store. *Oh, what I could have done with a bigger budget.*

Ava found a pair as sparkly as her dress, but silver and strappy as all get out. Katie's were a lovely simplistic pair of nude pumps with an ankle strap. Mine were somewhere in between. Strappy, but less than Ava's. Sparkly, but in a soft gold that would match the earrings I planned to wear that night.

Even Klare found shoes, which were brilliant, navy blue converse that would match her blue tuxedo. All of it a few shades darker than Ava's dress, to match, but almost look black until it hit the light just right. She had good taste. I couldn't wait to see her all dressed up.

"I swear, you two are going to be the envy of everyone else in the room. You're going to look amazing together," I told both Ava and Klare.

A smile lit up Ava's face.

"I think so too," she replied, looping an arm through Klare's.

We walked out of the shoe store with our purchases and headed to a nearby cafe to grab something quick to eat and maybe a cup of coffee. There were still a few hours before my date with August, and Katie didn't have to leave until later that night, so we figured we'd spend a little more time together.

It was a light-hearted afternoon spent talking about

things unrelated to the Dating Experiment and the Reveal Ball for once. I found out that Katie was an illustration major in college, and was only a year away from getting her Bachelor's. I reminisced about college and told her that I was glad that part of my life was over. I felt so much more free out in the real world, even if I hadn't done much with that freedom until now.

Speaking of which.

My date that evening was a bike ride with August once he got off of work. Technically, it was his thing, but I sort of cheated and picked this activity specifically because he had previously told me he liked it. I know. Not playing by the rules much in the end here, but I wasn't sure they really mattered as much by that point. There was only one more day standing between us and the day of the Ball.

I brought him a coffee that I had gotten to-go from the Cafe earlier as a gift. We didn't talk much on this date, which was fine by me. August was used to the exercise, I was not. Talking would have only made me run out of breath. As it was, my legs were getting sore by the time we made it halfway around the park.

I only struggled to keep up a little bit, though, so I guess there's that. And, August only laughed at me a little...

"Hey, you have to give me some credit here," I said as we pulled off to the side of the bike path and came to a stop. "For not riding a bike in I don't know how long, I think I did pretty well."

He chuckled lightly.

"No. You're right. You did great."

We parked our bikes up against a nearby bench and sat down.

"It's going to be weird... when all of this is over," he said.

"What do you mean?"

"Well, think about it. Even if we stay together, it's not going to be like this afterward. We're going to go back to working full-time, living our lives, doing whatever we used to do before. We're not going to see each other every day."

"I guess I hadn't thought of it like that," I admitted.

"It's odd to think about, isn't it? It's like you've just become this fixture of my days, something I can count on, expect."

"I know exactly what you mean."

Well, now that he had so kindly pointed it out, there my brain went, dealing with the reality of this new situation. There were days I wasn't going to see him and, all of a sudden, I missed him already, even though he was right next to me. My brain was yelling "*Hold on to him while you can!*"

This is normal, though, I told myself. Normal people have relationships where they don't see each other every day. We're just going to be a normal couple for once. Yet it still hurt a little to think about it.

"I wonder if everyone else is feeling that way too," I said.

He shrugged.

"I don't know how likely that is, but I'd like to hope so. I'd like to hope that at least some of them are, because that means this whole thing worked the way it was supposed to, right? I want to believe at least some of the other couples have made a connection like ours."

I smiled at his words. *A connection like ours*. We were the good example. We were the high bar. We were the kind of couple they'd post on their ads to entice more singles to sign up. That's what my life had turned into. I was that girl. How did I get so lucky? It seemed too good to be true, like something out of a fairy tale, or a cheesy romance novel, even if August wasn't some broad-chested, tan-skinned Adonis of a man.

How was I, of all people, part of the poster couple for dating success?

SMOKEY EYES WITH SYRUP

OUR LAST DATE before the Reveal Ball was a simple affair. We watched movies, ate popcorn, and cuddled on his couch with Luna lying across our laps.

Then came the madness.

Wednesday morning Ava rushed into my bedroom and jumped on the bed, bouncing and yelling at me to wake up.

"Come on, come on! We gotta go get our hair done!"

I groaned and shielded my eyes from the sunlight streaming through my windows, which she must have opened before assaulting me.

"Alright, alright. Just give me a moment, would ya?"

She hopped off the bed and retreated back into her own bedroom, while I forced myself to at least sit up. I could have killed her for scheduling our appointments so early in the morning, as it was only 8:00. She was my sister, though, so I refrained. She was lucky I loved her.

I did my rounds with Cinnabun, making sure she was all

set to go, and asked one of our friendlier neighbors to look after her as I expected we'd both be out all day and into the night. I even told the woman to give Cinnabun extra treats for me today, so she might not miss me as much.

"Oh! I almost forgot!" Ava called out before she came hopping into my bedroom, pulling her pants up with a wiggle and a grunt. "I may have also scheduled us to have our makeup and nails done as well, so like, be prepared for that."

I rolled my eyes. Typical.

"I suppose at this point I don't really have another choice," I argued.

She smiled devilishly.

"That may be why I 'forgot' to mention it until now?"

I would have expected nothing less.

She drove us to the salon in her pre-owned, baby blue Ford Focus. When we got there the place was already busy. Almost every chair was filled.

"Ava and Ella Carter?" asked a petite blonde behind the reception desk. Ava nodded. "Alright, follow me then. Ava, you'll be with Shannon. Ella, you'll be with Lacey." (Yay!)

She led us over to two chairs right next to each other and Lacey came out to consult with me.

"Everyone seems to have wanted to get in early today,"

Lacey told me as she washed my hair. "You'd think it was prom season."

There were only fourteen woman total in the Dating Experiment. Had all of them decided to come to this one place?

"There's a Ball tonight," I informed her.

Her face lit up.

"Oh! You know, you're absolutely right!" Lacey had a small southern twang that sounded easy on my ears. "Where has my memory gone. We typically get this at the end of each month, but I've been so busy with the new baby that I'd forget my name if it weren't pinned to my work shirt."

"Oh my, God! Congratulations! I'm so sorry I completely forgot about the baby. It's been a whirlwind of a time for me too lately."

"Thank you, Sweetheart," she said with a smile. "And that's okay."

"Why are there so many women, though? There aren't that many of us participating in the Dating Experiment each month."

"Oh, but don't you know, those girls they got working for them have to dress up too. And the guys. It's not just the daters that get to participate in the ball. It's the staff as well."

That made sense. Somehow, I hadn't even considered the

staff. I wondered, briefly, what it was like to have to go to this Ball every month. Could you opt out? Was it fun even after the tenth time? I supposed maybe it could be. Back in college, people would go to parties every *weekend*. A month was plenty of time to get that party itch again.

Lacey had always loved working with my long, red hair and, eventually, we worked out a style that would look pretty and elegant, but still fit underneath the panda head for the beginning of the evening. She curled my hair and braided parts here and there, wrapping them around my head like a crown. Then she pulled out strands in various places to give it that messy, but purposefully so look. I liked it a lot.

When she was done, I turned my head to the left and right as far as I could manage to look at the sides, and she held up a small mirror behind me so that I could see the back in the *big* mirror.

"This is amazing! I love it!"

"I'm glad to hear that, Sweetie. You look beautiful!"

Lacey did my makeup as well. I'd asked her to give me a more natural look, as I wasn't about that heavy caked-on feeling, and she gave me exactly what I had imagined.

My lips were a soft pink. There was a small amount of eyeliner and mascara to make my eyes stand out a little more, and just enough blush to give my cheeks a little bit rosier of an appearance. She kept my freckles visible and otherwise made sure that I didn't have any redness that shouldn't have been there.

"And what color nail polish would you like?" she asked when we'd moved on.

I suggested a deep red that matched my dress.

All-in-all, when everything was said and done, I didn't think I looked much like myself. I mean... I did, but... I looked like a much prettier version of what I was used to seeing in the mirror. I looked like I could be a movie star. I smiled, taking it all in.

"O.M.G!" Ava came and stood beside me, looking in the mirror. "Look at my baby sister! You're all grown up!"

She fanned at her face and I could tell she was trying to stop tears from spilling over. My cheeks flushed. Why did she have to embarrass me like this?

"Um... yeah, okay," I responded. "Please don't cry, though?"

She inhaled deeply and let it back out slowly through her nose.

"I know, I know. I'm sorry. I can't ruin this makeup."

I turned and finally *looked* at her. She had this stunning smokey eye with her lids painted silver. Her lips, like mine, were a pale pink that complimented our fair skin tone. Her hair had been curled and partially tied up, with a silver, jeweled clip in the back holding it in place.

"You are going to be the shiniest thing in the room," I told her with a laugh. "But that's okay, because you deserve to shine."

Sappy, I know. I'm rolling my own eyes at myself.

We hugged briefly, careful not to mess each other's looks up. Now that everything was starting to come together, the excitement was growing. After all, first and foremost, this was a Ball. A dance. A party. It was going to be fun.

And since we had only been at the salon for about two hours, so it was still early in the day.

"You wanna get breakfast?" Ava asked. "We literally *never* get breakfast."

"Sure, but something easy and not so messy. I don't want to have to wipe my face or mouth and accidentally take off lipstick or something."

"Of course. I'm thinking that pancake place on 41st? Pancakes can be cut up and you can get them in all sorts of flavors with toppings."

"Sounds good."

I wasn't kidding when I joked to August that it was like we were back in high school going to prom. It was exactly like that. The same kind of excitement filled the air around us, and you know what was even better? I was experiencing it with my sister.

She had graduated just before my freshman year, so other than elementary school, we didn't get to experience much of the school stuff together. We were both there for each other for our individual proms, and even the lame little school dances, but never together. This felt so much more special.

"Mom and dad would love this," I quietly noted on the way to the pancake place. "We're gonna have to send them pictures and tell them all about it."

Ava smiled.

"We will when you bring August home and they ask how the two of you met."

"We're so sure that I'll be bringing August home someday?"

"Please, I've been around the two of you. He's perfect for you, Ella. You have to keep him. You must."

I laughed.

"Right, well, okay then. They'll get the whole story when I bring him home. What about you and Klare, though?"

She shrugged.

"I guess I might want to warn them that I'm into women first. See how that goes. Play it from there."

I nodded in agreement.

"I think they'll take it just fine, though. You know mom and dad. They're cool about that kind of thing."

"I know... that's what I hope for."

I reached over and held the hand she had rested on the middle console.

"Don't worry about it, Ava. I know they'll accept you no matter what. Just like I do."

She glanced over at me for a brief moment, a warm smile on her face.

"Okay, but please stop now," she said with a laugh. "If you start getting all sappy on me I'm going to cry and ruin my makeup."

DANCE THE NIGHT AWAY

I TAKE IN a deep breath, let it out slowly. We're in a freaking *stretch limo*! The lights are this beautiful purple-blue, and there's a bar, and we've got some upbeat music going. I'm sitting between Katie and Ava, since they picked up all of us girls in the one vehicle. I can't believe it. I've never been in a limo before. My jaw practically hit the floor when it pulled up and beeped for us outside of our apartment.

We were all talking over each other, too excited to contain ourselves. I felt like I was lighter than air, floating on a soft, fluffy cloud of euphoria. As I looked around, I could see a glow on the faces of the women around me. Everyone's smiles were so bright, their eyes shining. I imagined I must have looked the same.

We pulled up to the Center and put our masks on. There, waiting by the other entrance, was the men's car. My heart pounded in my chest knowing that August was in that limo, all dressed up in his tux, ready to see me soon, really, truly see me. I bet he looked handsome as hell in that tux.

The Dating Experiment

The driver came and opened the door and, one by one, we climbed out as he held our hands. The men, much rowdier than us, were getting out as well, some of them practically leaping out of the limousine. A few of the women around me giggled at this, but I stared, waiting to see the koala head poke out. When it did, he looked my way and gave me a small wave. I smiled big, but was ushered forward before I remembered he couldn't see it. (I should have waved back.)

We bundled into the elevators to the ballroom floor and, once the doors slid open, we were in a whole new world. Everything shimmered and shined. The hardwood floor was a dark walnut and the tiled dance floor, which took up most of the space, was cream and gold. The gold glittered in the light of the chandeliers hanging above our heads.

The walls of the ballroom where cream and accentuated with gold. The curtains in the window, however, were a deep red that matched my dress. The ceiling was high and arched at the top, and there were tables with food and drinks lined up against one wall. A live band was set up on stage in the far corner. There were tables scattered about the wooden floor.

Warm hands wrapped around my waist from behind.

"Good evening, Miss Carter."

August's low voice came close to where my ear was

underneath the panda head, and I leaned into him, the smile on my face stretching from ear to ear. I closed my eyes for a moment to let everything sink in without getting too overwhelmed.

"Good evening, Dr. LaMarche," I responded, my voice low, as sultry as I could manage being mostly an inexperienced, awkward person.

He chuckled softly.

"I like the way that sounds rolling off your lips."

My skin flushed. I could feel it. I liked the way it sounded too. I liked saying it.

He took my hand and led me out to the dance floor where other couples were culminating. The show runner, Holly Van Warden, took the microphone set up for the lead singer. We all turned to face her. She was dressed impeccably in a shimmering gold dress that was fitted to her body. She sparkled under the colored lights of the stage.

"Good evening Ladies and Gentlemen," she began. "It is my utmost pleasure to welcome you to our favorite event of the month, the Reveal Ball!" There was clapping. A few people cheered. "It is my sincere hope that all of you have enjoyed this month-long ride as much as we intended for you, and that you've found someone worthy of sharing a future with.

"As you may or may not know, the first half of this evening

you will remain masked, but after the intermission it will be time to remove them!" A few more cheers. "We know that you're all bubbly with anticipation, and so are we! As always, this is the part where we see the connections people have really come to life. We hope you have a wonderful evening and a bright future to come!"

Once Holly left the stage, the band members came out and started their first set. Before I was willing to dance, though, I pulled August over to one of the tables to grab a glass of champagne. I needed a little added confidence, even after all of my work with Katie.

"Your dress is absolutely beautiful," August commented when we were far enough away from the band to hear a little better.

"Thank you."

I handed him a glass. I had been right, by the way. His tall, slender frame looked absolutely gorgeous in a fitted tux. Unfortunately for me, he totally caught me checking him out.

"Enjoying the view, huh?"

I lightly smacked his arm and he laughed. After downing the champagne, I let him lead me back out onto the dance floor. The band was still playing a more upbeat song, and so it was easier for me to get into this one. I didn't have to worry about messing up any moves. To my horror, however, August decided that embarrassing the shit out of me was the best way to start this night off.

His arms were flailing. He shook his behind. His legs were all over the place. His dance moves caused other people to stare, and I couldn't help but cover my panda eyes, wishing I could slink away unnoticed.

"Oh my, God! Please stop!" I begged.

He laughed hard, but eventually stopped. Then, he reached forward to pull my hands away from the mask and brought me into a hug.

"What if that is actually how I dance and you've just gone and insulted me?"

I rolled my eyes.

"Then I've changed my mind. This has been fun and all, but..."

"Ouch!"

His body shook with another laugh. I loved the feeling of it, and of the sturdy but soft material of his jacket against my arms. I wanted to rest my head on his chest, (Not the damn panda one!) and listen to his heart beating softly, his breathing constant and even.

The next song was a slow one. He rested his "chin" on top

of the panda mask and held me to him as we swayed to the music. I had no idea where Ava, Katie, and Klare had gone off to, but at that moment I also didn't care. I didn't feel like I needed them to be comfortable in this situation I had never experienced before. August was enough.

"I'm so glad I let my sister talk me into this," I admitted.

"I am too. I mean, I'm glad *I* was talked into it, but I suppose I'm very glad that you were as well."

"You could be dancing with some other woman right now. That's such a weird thought to me."

"I could be, but I'm glad I'm not."

He always knew what to say to make me melt inside.

We continued to dance. a I felt as light as a feather in his arms the whole time. The band was good. They played a lot of classics, so most of the people seemed to know every song. It really helped keep people moving.

I was actually a bit surprised to see just how many people it took to put the Dating Experiment together. The room was filled beyond the twenty-six remaining participants. All of the workers were dressed up just as nice as we were, smiling just as brightly. It was all so awe-inspiring to see. It didn't feel like there could possibly a happier moment anywhere else in the world.

August was, when he was actually trying, a pretty good

dancer. He had no problem leading me around the floor, even though I was a little clumsier and unbalanced at times. He just held me tighter and helped to direct me.

"I swear I've got this ballroom dancing stuff down, though," I assured him. "I honestly thought that's what we would have done first."

I was slightly disappointed. All that practicing and I hadn't been able to show my moves off yet.

"That's our first dance after the intermission. Unmasked."

"Oh." My pulse quickened. "I suppose that does make sense."

And that made me more nervous. The butterflies in my stomach had butterflies. Now he would have a face to put to the dancer, and if I ended up a disaster after all, there was no hiding. I did my best to push the thought out of my head. It was something I could worry about later. Right then, in that moment, I was just having the time of my life.

DROPPING THE BALL

WITH FLUSHED AND glowing faces, we decided to take a break. Ava and Klare joined us at a table and we filled a large plate with all sorts of snacks to pick at. We also grabbed a few more glasses of champagne. As I had imagined, a lot of people had their eyes on Ava and Klare, curious looks about them.

"How does it feel?" I asked. "How has everything been going?"

August leaned back and laid his arm across the back of my chair. Ava and Klare were scooted together on their side.

"Amazing!" they both gushed in unison.

"This is probably the best coming out experience I could have asked for," Ava added with a laugh, causing the rest of us to laugh with her.

"I've got to hand it to you," said Klare. "You sure know how to step out of a closet."

More laughs. She was right, though. Ava was a glittering jewel amongst the crowd that night. I'd never seen my sister enjoying herself so much. Even if things didn't work out the way she had originally imagined they would, I was glad they worked out the way they did.

After snacking on chips and small cakes and plenty of those weirdly amazing mints that you only ever seem to find at wedding receptions, I decided I needed a quick bathroom break. I bumped my panda head against August's koala in a mock kiss before disappearing to the lady's room off to our left.

Katie was inside, talking to a few other woman at the mirror. They were de-masked, checking hair and makeup to make sure that the animal heads weren't messing everything up. I did my business and, when I came out of the stall, Katie was still standing at the mirror, waiting for me. I took the panda head off and held it by my side.

"Isn't this Ball amazing?" she asked. "I feel like I'm in a dream!"

I smiled. She looked perfect with her short, cropped curls in her pale pink dress. I couldn't tell if her cheeks were so rosy from the dancing or her makeup, but she looked so much like a porcelain doll at that moment.

"It is," I agreed.

"Are you nervous?" she asked.

"I-I guess maybe..."

I couldn't give a straight answer. Part of me was. Part of me wasn't. I was still trying to hold on to what August and I had talked about only a few days ago, when I'd confessed that I was afraid he'd walk away from me after all of this.

"I am," she whispered softly.

I tilted my head, confused.

"Why? Katie, you're so pretty. Any guy would be lucky to be here with you tonight. I don't think you have anything to worry about."

She blushed.

"Thanks. You're so sweet. I don't really know, though. I'm just... I'm afraid that I won't be... *enough*. Like... he'll look around and see the other women in the room, and one of them will look like a model, or a movie star, and he'll think that in comparison I'm just... okay."

I set the panda head down on the counter, grabbed her shoulders, and looked her right in the eye.

"Listen to me, Katie. If this guy is worth anything at all, if he's who you're meant to be here with, you will be the most beautiful woman in the room in his eyes. Remember, you've already formed a connection with him as a person. If he feels that too, he won't even bother to look at the other women in the room."

196

She gave me a shy smile and pulled me into a tight hug.

"You're the best person I've met this whole month, Ella. Thank you for being my friend. August is gonna love you. If he doesn't, imma march out there and kick that boys ass."

We both laughed, then she let go. I checked myself in the mirror as she went back out to find her date. Then I was back out in the ballroom myself, heading back to our table.

The music had stopped. Band members were getting drinks and mingling with the workers. The happy couples were snacking and chatting away. Some were still dancing slowly in the center of the room like there was a bit of music left over that only they could hear. I took my seat next to August.

"Intermission time?" I asked.

He nodded.

"Bathroom breaks, food, beverages, fresh air. Get it all now while you can."

"I think I might just be good right here," I responded, leaning into him.

He grabbed my hand and gave it a light squeeze. We all talked for a while. Ava gushed about Klare's dancing, as Klare apparently had some Michael Jackson worthy moves that she was hiding from the rest of us. Somehow, I didn't doubt that one bit.

When the intermission was coming to an end, Holly took

the stage again.

"How's everybody doing tonight?" she called into the mic. Cheers erupted all around the room. "Awesome! I'm so glad to hear that. We all are, here at the Dating Experiment headquarters! It's always fun to work with and get to know all of the participants each and every month. Sometimes we do get repeats, but most of you are new faces for us. It means a lot that you trust us with your love lives the way you do."

Queue laughter.

"So," she continued, "as you all know, the night is only halfway through, and that means we still have a lot of partying left to do. However, as you *also* know, it is finally time to shed those masks!" So much cheering from everyone. "I want all the lovely ladies to line up on one side of me, right out there on the dance floor. All the lovely men, stand here on my other side," she said, gesturing to her right. "Across from your lady."

We did as we were told, standing across from each other in two lines, about five feet apart. I looked across at August, my heart pounding in my chest, my hands starting to feel all sweaty and gross. I casually tried to wipe them on my dress without anyone noticing. If August had, I couldn't tell.

"Alright!" Holly called out. "On the count of one, take those masks off! Three... two..." (Insert unnecessarily long pause.)

"One!"

I sucked in a deep breath and reached up to lift the panda head off. I hadn't even realized I was squeezing my eyes shut until I couldn't see when the mask was off my head. I opened them, and my breath hitched. Just for a moment. Just a heartbeat. I set the panda head on the floor.

Across from me, August was still holding his koala head. We stepped toward each other, just like the other couples were doing. Up close, I took every detail of him in.

His eyes were pale green, the color of sage. His hair was a very light brown, curling on top of his head and cut short on the sides. He wore thin, wire-rimmed glasses. His lips were a thin line surrounded by his short, neatly trimmed facial hair. His face was narrow, with an angled jaw, and when he opened his mouth to potentially say something, I noticed the crooked front tooth at the bottom.

He did have streaks of gray running through his hair, and I wondered briefly how old he actually was, but then I pushed that thought away, because, honestly, it didn't matter to me. I'd always suspected we weren't the same age, and he still looked fairly young to me. People I had graduated high school with had gray hairs by this time already. It's different per person.

He was absolutely adorable, in this tall, slender, geeky

sort of way. He was cute. Super cute. The problem was, he had shut his mouth now, and still, nothing had come out. He wasn't saying anything. (Though neither was I, honestly.) He was just... staring at me.

I could feel my hands starting to sweat again.

"... August?" I asked cautiously.

He stepped forward, only inches from me, and put his palm to my cheek. I could feel the hesitation. His hand trembled as he ran his thumb over my skin. I didn't think much of it at first. I thought maybe this was a good sign. I thought maybe he was just at a loss of words, because maybe he thought I was cute too. But then...

His eyes dropped to the floor and his hand left my face. He stood very still for a moment and then... and then he just... walked away from me. I stood there, glued to my spot, watching his back retreating from me. He never looked back. He simply kept going. Across the room. Out the doors. And who knows where after that.

Remember when Katie said I'd be turning heads and that it was true, but I said I'd get back to that later? Well, now it was later, and everyone's eyes were on me. The room was dead silent and I could feel the same question in everyone's unspoken words.

What   just   happened?

NETFLIX AND BREAKFAST

I HADN'T SEEN anyone else walk out of the room. Just August. As I stood there, trying to comprehend everything, the world became a blur around me. I was aware of people beginning to move and speak to each other, but I couldn't hear what they were saying. My vision was becoming watery from the tears building up in my eyes.

I was so embarrassed.

Humiliated, really.

He... he assured me...

Someone was coming toward me, but I didn't stick around to wait for them. Instead, I turned around and walked out the same way August had gone. I wasn't chasing him. I didn't have hope that I'd even catch up. I just wanted to be out of that room and away from all the eyes of the happy people around me.

"Ella!"

I kept moving, even with my name being called in the background. It was a little on the chillier side, since it was later in the evening. I hadn't even thought to grab a coat. Of course.

"Ella!"

I felt like I was choking on the air somehow. My chest felt tight. Why would he do that? Why would he walk out on me like that? In front of everyone? What had I done wrong? Was he expecting something else? Did he not care what he'd said about us being friends if nothing else? It... it was like he wanted nothing to do with me.

I sank to my knees in the middle of the cold, hard sidewalk. People walking by had to move around me. Eventually, whoever was following caught up. They leaned down by my side. I felt a hand rest lightly on my back.

"Ella."

I looked over into Ava's shimmering eyes. Klare was coming up behind her, followed by Katie and, I assumed, Katie's date.

"I'm so sorry, Ella," Katie said from the back of the group.

Ava, noticing the tears silently pouring down my cheeks, pulled me into a hug.

"Everything's gonna be alright," she whispered into my ear. "I know it doesn't feel like it right now, but we'll... we'll figure this out."

"Yeah!" Katie agreed enthusiastically. "My offer still

stands. We kick this man's ass if he doesn't explain himself."

"Text him," Ava urged. "We'll start there. I'm sure there's a reason for why he walked out. It may not even be about you. I saw you guys together. You can't just... throw that kind of connection away."

I sniffed, wanting to believe she was right. When I got home again, I was going to text him right away.

"Alright if I take a bus back now?" I asked.

My voice was raspy. It came out quieter than I had intended. Ava nodded.

"I'll come with you."

"Me too," Klare agreed.

"Me three!" Katie added.

I shook my head at that one.

"No. Katie, you go back. I don't want to spoil this night for you. Ava's my sister, and I won't convince her otherwise, but you should go have fun. You and..."

"James."

"Right. You and James."

She gave me a sad look.

"Are you sure?"

I nodded slowly.

"One-hundred percent. I won't be happy if you stay with

me."

She sighed and grabbed James's hand.

"Let's go," she said, looking into his eyes. Turning back to me she said, "Text me too. I can come over tomorrow or something. If you want."

"Thanks. I'd like that."

I watched them walk away and I didn't feel jealous. Katie was such a nice girl. I was happy that she was having a good time. I couldn't take that away from her. Ava, Klare, and I walked to the bus station and then hitched a ride back to our apartment. I felt a little numb the whole ride.

-

It was two in the morning. I'd texted August right away when I got back, but he had never answered. I'd simply asked what happened and if everything was alright.

Now out of our fancy dresses and makeup, Ava, Klare, and I were bundled up on the couch in our pajamas, watching Netflix. Well, Klare was in a pair of Ava's pajamas, but same difference. Neither of them seemed to care about keeping me company so late while I couldn't sleep. Though, eventually, we did all fall asleep.

Netflix was still up, but nothing was playing. It was semi light outside, so I couldn't have been asleep for more than a few hours. My eyes burned, and my body was cramped from the position I had been curled up in. I stretched out and then sat up. Klare and Ava stirred beside me when I moved.

The first thing I did was check my phone, but there were no messages. No missed calls. My shoulders sank and I slumped back into the couch.

"Nothing, huh?" Ava asked. I shook my head. She got up and walked to the kitchen. "I'm gonna make some breakfast. Anything in particular you're in the mood for?"

I shook my head again. I wasn't really hungry.

Was I overreacting? Was I being childish? Clingy? What if something... something couldn't have come up, though. He hadn't received a call or a text. He'd just been looking at me. It had to be something about me, right? His face when he had looked at me, there was distress there. He saw something he didn't like. There was no other answer. Everything had been perfectly fine right up until that moment.

It was odd. For a brief moment I wanted him to comfort me, but then I remembered he was the reason I was upset in the first place.

"I'll make French toast," Ava finally decided. "I feel like we haven't had that in a while. I'll cut up some fruit, scramble any leftover eggs, and we have juice in the fridge. Sound good?"

"Sure."

Klare put a hand on my shoulder.

"I'm sorry, Ella."

"Thanks."

She gave me a half-hearted smile and then got up to use the bathroom. I bundled up in the blanket I had been using for the movie and rolled over onto my side. I couldn't help staring at my phone. *Come on, August. You must have a good reason for walking out on me like that.*

We ate breakfast. Klare and Ava were the ones to talk the most. I just kind of sat there, picking away at my food, watching my phone.

Katie texted me eventually.

Katie: Hey. I hope you're feeling alright. Want me to come over still? I don't have to if you don't want.

Me: You can come over. Any time. I'll be here all day.

Katie: Alright! You won't regret this. I promise. I thought of something that might cheer you up a little, even if it doesn't fix things.

Me: Oh?

Katie: You're not allowed to ask any questions.

This is gonna be a surprise. ;) I'll be over around noon.

Me: Ok... see you then.

What surprise thing could Katie have possibly had that could cheer me up? I tried to brainstorm all of the possibilities, but I couldn't come up with anything. When I asked Ava and Klare they both shrugged.

"I don't know her well enough," Ava admitted. "I have no clue what could be going on in that girl's head."

I could say the same. We weren't that close yet. I just hoped she was right. Maybe what I needed was something to take my mind off of everything until August answered me back. Something to keep me from checking my phone every two minutes. He was going to respond eventually. He had to.

WITCH WITH A CAPITAL B

LIKE CLOCKWORK, KATIE showed up at noon, right on the hour. In her arms she carried a large cardboard box filled with all sorts of things. I moved out of the way to let her in and she set the box down with a huff.

"Alright, I got stuff in here for like, a whole spa experience. It's something I do when I'm having a rough day. I have face masks, nail files, clippers, polish, lotion, a foot soaker, a lot of wine, and some other cool stuff."

"You really go all out, don't you," I commented.

She smiled, clearly very proud of herself.

"I've learned there's no better way to relax and cool down than to kick back and treat yourself." Her bubbly demeanor toned down. "I mean, I'm not always this happy-go-lucky. I'm human, like everyone else. You just haven't seen me having one of my bad days yet. So, shall we set up on the couch?"

I nodded and let her lead the way.

A short while later we were both sitting on the couch with

face masks on. I had my feet in the foot soaker, which pleasantly bubbled, and Katie currently had her hands in heated pads. In front of us, a baking competition was playing on the TV. Ava and Klare had joined us for the face mask portion, and we all sat in our pajamas.

Wine was poured. Boxes of chocolate sat between us. Per Katie's demands, phones were not only put away, but turned off. Candles on the coffee table gave off the sweet scent of warm, baking cookies, making our stomachs quickly rumble.

"Pizza?" Katie asked.

I nodded.

"The largest pepperoni pizza we can order."

She laughed as Ava dug out the menu we kept around with all of the fast food and delivery places in the city listed.

"Joe's has a twenty-four inch," she announced once she found the place.

"Let's do that one, then."

She was allowed her phone for this one instance and dialed away.

"I added cheesy bread too," she told us as she came back to the living room, much to our approval.

So we ate, drank and, once I'd changed the water in the foot soaker and done my collagen rub, Katie and I traded treatments. I took the red nail polish off and picked a new color for when we begin to paint them, because right then I didn't want to look at that shade of red. I picked a bright and cheery bubble gum pink instead.

By the end of the day, I had painted fingers and toenails, soft, glowing skin, and I was so relaxed I wanted to fall asleep on the couch again. Katie stayed for dinner and then dessert. We made ourselves ice cream Sundays and found a movie to watch. She didn't leave until around eleven that night.

"I have to be at work pretty early in the morning, otherwise I'd love to stay the night," she responded when we'd offered for her to stay.

She had a point. I actually had to work early that Friday morning as well. It was best for both of us if she went home and we both got some sleep.

My phone was lying on my bed. As I walked up to it there was an overwhelming feeling of apprehension growing in the pit of my stomach. What if he still hadn't answered me? What if he had, but the answer was something that I really didn't want to hear? (Read?) There was the slight possibility that I was actually better off not knowing.

I picked it up and hit the "On" button anyway, and then had to wait for it to reboot. In the dead silence of my room, I could hear Ava and Klare having a muffled conversation out on the couch. Cinnabun was asleep.   The wait was killing me.

And then in turned on.

And there was nothing.

No messages waiting for me.

I Googled whether or not I would still be able to receive messages if my phone was off just to make sure and, sure enough, they would have still reached me once I turned it back on. So, in conclusion, it had been a whole day and August still hadn't bothered to answer me back.

It's okay, I told myself. *He may just need time. I can wait.*

I walked back out into the living room and plopped onto the couch next to Ava.

"Anything?" she asked.

I shook my head and she gave my shoulder a squeeze.

-

I went in to work the next morning and did my best not to screw up any of my designs from being too distracted. Shannon noticed that something was off and, of course, she had a good guess as to what it was about. I mean, she knew about the whole Dating Experiment gig after all. Thankfully, she did not push me when I told her I wasn't in the mood to talk about it. She simply told me that it was okay, as long as I thought I could still do my work just fine.

And I did, for the most part. I wasted some fondant, but not too much, and I dropped my cutter on the floor at least a handful of times. Other than that, I stayed in the back and worked quietly, not having a whole lot to do with anyone else in the store.

August was right. My first official day without him had felt... odd. It had felt like there was something missing. I'm just not sure if that was because he wasn't around, or because he wasn't around *and* he had walked out on me. Was it more about not knowing whether or not he would be back at all? And what if he wasn't? What if the night of the Reveal Ball was the last time I'd ever get to see him?

Ouch. Okay. That was a thought I needed to push out of my head right away, or I was going to break down right in the middle of making the fondant butterfly wings. Plus, I was baking today, so I needed to have my focus on listening for the cupcake timer. August wasn't going to be the reason I destroyed a whole batch of perfectly good cupcakes. I mean, at *that* point, he might as well be a monster.

The day wore on slowly. I left at 1:00 p.m. and, for the first time in a long time, had no idea what to do with myself. Ava was at work. Katie was at work. I had a whole bunch of free time that I wasn't used to having anymore.

I walked to the closest coffee house I could find and pulled out the book I usually carried around with me in my bag. Not a lot of people were in this coffee house, surprisingly. I had worried it was going to be busy at lunch time, since you could also get food from them.

But it was quiet.

I ordered a hot chocolate with whipped cream and then curled up in one of the large, soft armchairs in the back. I was about three-quarters of the way done with this current book, and the leading female character was turning into a real... witch with a capital B.

Interestingly enough, the main male character could see through her behavior and knew she must have been going through a rough time, so he forgave her. Odd, because all I could think while reading this book so far was man, you need to find yourself a new woman. This one's crazy!

So, she ended up shutting him out for, like, a whole week, but in the end he went over to her house with flowers and she was happy so they talked and now everything was good. Being that there was still more to the book, I didn't believe this was the last of her crazy, though. I couldn't wait to see what this poor guy would have to put up with next.

I'M NOT ANIMAL, BUT YOU'LL STILL
WANT TO SEE ME

IT HAD NOW been a full week. I had sent him another text message when I got home from the coffee house on Thursday, wondering if for some reason he hadn't gotten the first one. Maybe I was worried for nothing, after all.

Me: Hey. If you get this please call or text or... something. I'd really like to talk to you.

What did I get after that? Still nothing, even after another two days. Honestly, there was a part of me that wanted to lie in bed and sulk about it for the next month, at least. But then there was some stubborn part of me that needed an answer. If anything, if he wanted to leave me, fine. He could. I wanted some kind of closure, though. I wanted to hear him tell me, to my face, that he didn't want to see me anymore.

I thought back to the book I had read in the coffee house and, maybe that's why the idea came to me, but I knew what I had to do. At first I had tried his apartment, but he wasn't there, so I pulled out my phone and looked for a Dr. LaMarche in the West Bay City area. His vet clinic was on the other side of the city. Not a problem.

I hopped on the first bus I could catch. It was rather packed for a Friday afternoon. Did any of these people have work? Of course, I wasn't working either, so who was I to judge, in all honesty? Still... too many people. I was nervous enough and didn't need to add feeling smothered. Any one of these people, or more, could have been at the ball that night, whether worker or participant. It made me feel as though some of them were watching me.

I tried really hard to keep my breathing even and under control, which I think weirded out those who were near me, because they kept giving me strange looks. (I'm not dying, guys, I'm just... panicking a little.) Who wouldn't be in my situation? What if August wasn't at work either? Maybe he was just gone somewhere. I hadn't even thought to check the park where he could have been out with Luna.

The bus pulled into the station and I climbed off with a mass of people as another mass waited to board. The clinic was only about a five-minute walk from the station. If I was smarter, like Ava, I would get my own car. I had a license. It's not like there was anything stopping me.

On the way I passed a lot of other neat places I'd never been to before. There was a really cool looking vintage and antique store that I told myself I was going to need to come back to sometime in the future. There was also a record store, an ice cream shop, a barber, and a flower shop. I noticed that it was a very quiet little area, where the buildings weren't so tall, and people lived in lower quality apartments. Although, they were still alright looking to me. This wasn't the sketchy part of the city yet.

I found the little, white office building between a hardware store and, conveniently, if I must say so myself, a pet goods store. I bet every person that went to August's vet clinic felt inclined to by their pet a toy or a treat when they left their appointment. That store must have been doing well.

I stood out on the street for a moment, contemplating what I was actually about to do. (If he was there.) I would never have called myself a particularly brave person. Maybe sometimes a little crazy, and this could have easily fallen into the latter category, but I did *feel* brave at least, at that moment. So, I took that feeling and I worked with it, marching right into the little building and right up to the front desk.

"Hi, do you have an... appointment today?"

The woman at the desk looked around for an animal and, when she couldn't find one, looked a little confused as she asked the question.

"Actually, no, but I was wondering if um..." *Deep breaths, Ella.* "I was wondering if Dr. LaMarche is in today."

"He is."

Really? That's all I get? You think I'm just gonna be all "Great, thanks! Now I can go!" Come on, lady.

"Is he... busy?"

"He's actually on his lunch break at the moment. Is there something you need to speak with him about? A question? If you'd like, I could schedule an appointment for you. What kind of animal is this visit in regards to?"

I sighed. Okay. Fine.

"Actually, this is a personal matter. It's... a family thing. I just don't know if he would feel comfortable with me giving you the details, as, you know, they're a bit personal. Tell him it's Ella."

"Alright... wait right here and I'll go see if he has a moment."

You literally just said he was eating lunch...

She disappeared behind a door. There were two other people in the lobby, one of them sitting with a cat. The cat was not in a carrier like you'd expect. It was on a leash. This fascinated me more than it should have, especially because I was supposed to be focusing on the fact that I was here for a very serious reason.

"Ella..."

I whipped around at the sound of his voice. There he was, in his vet attire, looking every bit as cute as he had the night of the Ball. For a moment, I forgot everything. I forgot how hurt and angry I was. All I could think was "that's *my* August. The man I was so used to having around me now. The man I had missed." Of course, he wasn't mine anymore... not really. Not like he had been.

He nodded to the receptionist and she retreated behind the front desk. Then he gestured for me to go outside, so I did, with him following close behind.

"What are you doing here?" he asked once the door closed behind us.

"Whoa there. You are not the one who gets to ask the questions here, August." Where was this edge in my voice coming from? "You don't get to inquire about *why* I'm doing what I'm doing or *where* I'm doing it. You're the one who needs to be *answering* the questions."

"Ella, now is not rea..."

"Oh no! I'm not done yet. Let me finish. I didn't come here because I *need* you, if that's what you're worried about. I didn't come here to try and *beg* for you back. I came here, because I want answers. I want to know why you did what you did. Do you know what happened after you left? Of course you don't, because you weren't there. I was, though. I was still standing in that same *damn* spot.

"I was there for the awkward silence that followed. I was there for all of the eyes staring in my direction. I was there for the whispers I'm sure were happening, but I couldn't actually hear them, because I was so discombobulated that everything sounded hazy and far away. I was there when everyone started to go back to normal, because that's really the only thing they could do. Then I was gone too.

"But for the shittiest part of the night, August, I was there. Why? After everything, after we'd talked and you reassured me... why would you walk out on me like that?"

He rubbed at his arm in a nervous way. He wasn't even looking at me anymore. He was looking at something in the grass. At first, I didn't think he was going to respond, because he was silent for so long. Then he did finally look back into my eyes.

"I'm sorry, Ella. Really, I am. This isn't how I wanted things to go. I just... I have to get back to work."

"Please... just give me closure so I can move on... just tell me *why*."

He looked at me for a moment longer. I could practically

see the thoughts swirling around inside his brain. If he thought any harder, there would be steam coming out of his ears.

"I'm sorry."

That was all he said. That was all he had for me. Afterward, he walked back into the clinic and left me standing behind. Yet again. I was once again in a daze until the glass doors shut with a bang, snapping me out of it.

What had I done to not even deserve so much as an answer?

HEAVY STUFF, MAN

I THOUGHT CONFRONTING him would do something, something immediate, but that didn't turn out to be the case. He still hadn't texted or called me in another three days, and now it was my time to sulk the way I truly wanted to. On my next day off of work, I didn't bother getting out of bed.

Ava took care of Cinnabun for me. She tried to take care of me too, but I wasn't having it for the most part.

"Come on," she said. "You need to at least eat something. I've made toast and eggs for breakfast. It's something simple. You can handle that, right?"

"Mmm."

She sighed and left the room. A moment later she came back with the eggs and toast, setting them on the bedside table.

"In any case, they're here if you want them. Just don't let the eggs sit too long, okay?"

"Mm."

My eyes were dry and they burned because of that. Crying through the night and not getting any sleep made me feel groggy and hopeless. The way he had dismissed me so easily. He walked away *again*. It was like a repeat of the Reveal Ball. He left me standing there looking and feeling like an idiot as he walked away from me. What a jerk? It just... it seemed so unlike him. I was hurt, and I was mad, but I also just could not wrap my head around the whole situation.

Maybe that was why I was mad.

I'd told Katie about confronting him. She was proud of me. I'd yet to tell her how that went, though. I left her message on read, thinking that eventually she'd take the hint. I didn't even want to talk to anyone at the time. I just wanted to be alone. I wanted to let out every negative thing I was thinking and feeling in privacy. I could deal with other people at a later time.

Ava came back after a while to remove the plate of untouched food. Then, against my heavy growls of disapproval, she opened up my curtains to let all the mocking sunshine in. I didn't want that. I didn't want all that warmth and cheeriness rubbing its happiness in my face. I didn't want to be reminded of everyone that was probably out enjoying this beautiful end of summer day while I was in my room, in pain.

"Your hair is going to be a tangled mess."

"Don't care."

"You need to shower. It'll help."

"Don't care."

"You have to go to work again tomorrow."

"Not my problem today."

"Ella."

"Leave me alone, Ava. Please!"

She sighed and left the room, but I knew she would be back again later. In fact, after her work shift, she came barreling through the front door and into my bedroom. In her hands were bags of delicious smelling food wrapped up in white boxes. Chinese. I groaned. She knew I couldn't pass that up.

"You don't even have to move," she said. "I'm gonna go get some plates and forks from the kitchen. Just wait here."

I waited. Sort of. While she was in the kitchen I snuck an egg roll and was just stuffing a second piece of sweet and sour chicken into my mouth when she reappeared.

"You don't get to gloat about this," I warned her. "You cheated by using a weakness of mine."

She laughed, but when she sat down on my bed her look turned serious.

"Look, I just want to talk to you, Ell. I know this royally sucks, and I'm sorry August hurt you the way that he did. I just want you to know that I'm sorry. I truly am."

"For what?"

"This is my fault. I'm the one that signed you up for this. You never would have done it if I hadn't practically forced you."

I shook my head.

"But you had no way of knowing how things would play out. You could never have known that he would walk out on me like that. After everything."

She shrugged.

"I know, but there's a part of me, deep down, that can't forgive myself right now. I know this is delving into that sappy part of our relationship that we try to avoid, but... I'm your big sister, Ella. It was my job since the very day you were born to watch out for you. I'm supposed to keep you safe. I'm not supposed to let you get hurt."

"That may have been the case when we were children, Ava, and I know you'll always have my back as an adult, but that's just it. I'm an adult. I could have said no. I could have backed out. I didn't. I made my own choices and, sure, maybe this was your idea overall, but I stuck with it. I'm not a kid. You're not always going to be able to protect me from getting hurt anymore, because I'm old enough to live my life the way I want to live it.

"Sometimes ... sometimes things aren't going to work out the way I want them to. But that's not your fault. That's not something you have to ever feel responsible for. Do you understand that? You can care about me. You can do your best to be my big sister. But sometimes I'm gonna make my own decisions and they aren't gonna work out in my favor and you'll have to accept that. Just... be there for me when that happens."

"I've been trying," she pointed out.

"Yeah. I know. Being there for someone also means giving them their space, though," I said with a nudge to her shoulder.

She smiled.

"I know. Deep down I've always known that. It's these maternal instincts I've been having lately. It's why I want to settle down. Some part of my brain wants to treat you like a child still, because that same part of me wants to be a mom. I'm not our mother, though. I'm your sister."

"My best friend."

She smiled even wider.

"Exactly."

"But I've learned something from all of this, you know?"

She cocked her head to the side.

"And what is that?"

"This world has so much more to offer me than what I've been giving it credit for. After this, I don't think I can go back to being an apartment hermit whose leaving only ever consists of going to work."

She laughed at this.

"Well, duh! That's only what I've been trying to tell you since you moved in with me! And you know what, Ella? You also have so much to offer the world. If August can't handle you for whatever reason, there are so many men out there who I'm sure could. You're beautiful, you're a talented artist, and you're one of the sweetest people I know. His loss."

"I think I can see that now," I replied. "I don't have to be so afraid of getting out and meeting people. I just did it, three times, and even if it didn't work out the way I wanted it to, it did show me that I'm a likable person, and that dating can be fun. There are lots of different kinds of people in this world. I really need to start meeting some of them."

"Proud big sister moment!"

I rolled my eyes.

"Yeah, whatever. You get what I'm saying, though, right? Look at how much good you've done me? You don't need to worry at all about this one bad thing. You helped me open up more regardless of my relationship status."

"Ooh! And you *did* finally get laid. So... points for me, because that goal was achieved."

"Yeah... okay... and the sisterly bonding moment is officially *over* now."

She laughed, but I didn't. Why do big sisters have to embarrass you like that sometimes? We were NOT going to talk about it, Ava!

YOU'RE A GODDAMN CREEPER

THE NEXT DAY, somewhat reluctantly, I got out of bed to get ready for work. I still hadn't slept well, and therefore was just as groggy and tired as the day before. I showered and got dressed in clothes that were at least clean, if not wrinkly for my lack of putting them away in their proper place. Not like it mattered. I planned to be in the back of the shop for my whole shift anyway. I wasn't ready to deal with happy customers yet.

Ava left a box of banana nut muffins on the table, so I grabbed one and a glass of orange juice, gulped the juice down in one go, and headed for the door. Just as my hand was reaching for the knob, my phone buzzed in my pocket. Rolling my eyes, I reached in and pulled it out, wondering who would text me at this hour.

It was August.

I fumbled with the phone to keep from dropping it out of sheer surprise.

August: I'm going to be down in the park later. If you're free. Sometime around 2:00-ish.

My heart immediately started hammering away. I couldn't think of anything to say, so I didn't respond. Maybe a small part of me even wanted to make him sweat it out, I don't know. Instead, I went to work, where I thought about nothing but that text message the whole time.

-

I have to go.

He clearly wants to talk, finally.

I need to hear what he has to say.

I need closure.

What if he says something I don't want to hear?

Maybe I should stand him up, payback for leaving me.

I don't think I'm that kind of person, though.

What would Ava want me to do?

Katie?

What do I want to do?

He may have realized he was wrong to walk away.

He may want to get back together.

Do I want to give him that second chance? No... scratch that. Of course I do.

The Dating Experiment

Does he deserve it, though?

-

I hung up my apron, washed myself up a bit, and said good-bye to Shannon for the day. It was only 1:00 p.m. I still had an hour before August was expecting me to potentially show up in the park. I walked around the streets aimlessly in the meantime, picked up a cup of coffee, and then headed in the general park direction.

I watched ducks swimming in a pond, children playing with their parents, riders on bikes whizzing past, and listened to all of the noise from these various things filling my ears at once. It was a sunny day, and surprisingly warm for nearing the middle of September. It would be fall soon, after all. I was already working on my fall cookie decorations for the bakery.

I finally saw August sitting on a bench by himself, no Luna. Instead, he was reading a book. For a moment, I could do nothing more than stand there and watch him, wondering what was going on in his head. How did he look so relaxed? Was that a good or a bad sign? Only one way to find out.

I walked up hesitantly, quietly. In the process I accidentally startled him. With a jump, he closed his book and set it to the side.

"Ella!"

I sat down on the bench next to him, but I didn't sit too close. I wasn't sure what this meeting was about, even though I wanted to lean into him and feel the comfort of being near again. I resisted the urge as best as I could. He turned to me, but I kept my eyes forward, on the grass.

"You finally want to talk?" I asked.

"Yes. Can you at least look at me, though?"

"Tell me why I'm here, first."

He sighed.

"Understandable... you're here... because I want to apologize."

Butterflies fluttered away in my stomach. My eyes stung with the effort of holding back tears. Finally, I turned to him. It was weird being so close, face to face, no mask. I had only been there once before, right before he had walked out on me. Now, however, he stayed, and I could see that there were dark circles under his somewhat bloodshot eyes. His hair was disheveled.

"You do?" He nodded, a solemn expression on his face. "What if I don't want to forgive you?" I asked.

His whole body tensed.

"I... suppose I would have to accept that, but please, just... hear me out."

He was quiet, as though waiting for me to respond.

"Well then, I'm listening."

My voice may have sounded cold and indifferent, but there were no such feelings on the inside. I was a raging pool of emotions, all of them, swirling together until I could no longer tell what exactly I was feeling at any given moment.

"I'm sorry. I don't think I can ever say that enough. I never should have walked out on you, Ella. It was a stupid thing to do. It was stupid and it was because I didn't think... I just... acted. On fear."

"What could you have possibly been afraid of?" I questioned.

"Everything." He leaned back on the bench and reached for my hand. Without thinking, I gave it to him and we sat side by side, both now staring out at the rest of the park. "Stupid stuff, mostly," he continued. "I turned forty just before this whole thing started. July twenty-fifth, to be exact. That was part of the reason I was pushed into the Dating Experiment in the first place. I wasn't getting any younger, and everyone around me agreed that I needed to settle down and find someone. I just... didn't know how, because that's not something I've ever been good at. So I paid the fee, I filled out the application, I showed up after being told it was for my best.

"I didn't know what all to expect, like most, I guess. I did know one thing, though, and that was that they had asked for my input on what I was looking for. Because I'm forty now... I told them I wasn't comfortable with anyone under the age of thirty."

"Oh... shit."

He nodded, but there was a smile on his face.

"I could tell immediately that you either looked incredibly young for your age, or they had gone against what I'd asked for, and me being me, assumed it had to be the latter."

"They did, though. You were right. I'm only twenty-six."

"Yes, but... I shouldn't have taken that out on you. You didn't lie to me, Ella, and I had reacted like I thought it was your fault. Like... maybe you did put a different age on your application."

"I never lied."

"I realized that...."

"If you don't mind me asking, why does this matter to you? I thought... I guess I just thought that we connected so well..."

He squeezed my hand a little tighter.

"It wasn't about you, or how old you were. Not really. It's always been about me."

"Did you really just 'It's not you. It's me?' as an explanation?"

I looked at him this time and he rolled his eyes.

"Well, yes, but we're not breaking up, so it's different."

"We're not?"

He tensed, then looked me in the eye.

"I mean, I'd like not to. I made a dumb choice, and I will get down on the ground and beg for your forgiveness if you want. The thing is, I'm just not... some days I still feel like I'm twenty again, and some days I'm reminded that I'm definitely not. The Reveal Ball was one of the latter days. All of a sudden, my being forty seemed so... old. And it's not. Not really. But it feels like it is. It feels like you're crossing a line and everything after that is just... it's happening too quickly. You've hit a point of no return and you're life's gonna come to an end, and you better know what you're going to do with the time you have left.

"I haven't accepted it yet. I don't want to feel old. I don't want people to look at me with you and think there's something wrong with either one of us. I don't want society to see me as this old man creeping on a younger woman. I don't want to feel like I *am*. And yet, that's the next thing I thought of at that moment, when you took the mask off. All I could think was... you're a goddamn creep for liking this girl, and she's gonna see it too. You can't give her a normal relationship."

"What changed your mind then?"

He looked down at our hands intertwined.

"I realized that none of that mattered, especially what other people think. I hadn't connected so well with anyone before, and that *did* matter. I realized that this doesn't change things. You are an adult. There's a lot we have in common. Getting married, having children, we can still do that... if you want. I'm not taking any of that away from you. Just because I've recently crossed over from a perfectly happy thirty-nine to a somehow much older sounding forty, doesn't mean I've suddenly become useless and unworthy."

"I'm sorry you felt that way. I never would have guessed... we even talked about children. You said you wanted them, so... how did that suddenly become a problem?"

"I guess I originally figured they wouldn't necessarily be my own. I could have adopted older children, so that I didn't feel like I'd be too old while they were growing up. I came to my senses, though, thankfully. I have the energy of a twenty-year-old," he said with a chuckle. "I don't think I'd have any problem chasing a toddler around."

I smiled, but there was one more thing I needed to ask.

"Why were you so cold when I confronted you at work?"

He looked away, out at the other people in the park.

"I'm ashamed of that. Honestly. I just... I don't know. I was right in the middle of the war in my head, because believe it or not, walking away from you was an instantly regretted decision. I hadn't wanted to. It felt like the rest of my body had responded with 'flight' before my brain had the chance to say stay and 'fight.' Panic took over. I missed you, though. I wanted to go back. Everything felt so conflicted and I was losing sleep.

"Actually, I did. I 'd stayed in the area. I was walking around the building and I did go back. By then you'd already left, but I'd understood. I hurt you. Why would you have stayed and waited for my dumb ass to come walking back through the door?"

I nodded, not disagreeing with the "dumb ass" that he had thrown in.

"I don't *completely* blame you. I probably shouldn't have shown up at your place of work. Maybe that was a little immature on my part. I'm sorry. Just... promise me you'll never leave me like that again."

He turned to face me and grabbed both of my hands, looking me right in the eye with a serious expression.

"I promise I will never leave you like that again. I sincerely hope that you can forgive me. I was an asshole. And I'm sorry. And... I love you, Ella.

"And you went back.

"I did."

I sat for a moment, contemplating. Then I finally

responded.

"I love you too."

Think what you want. Maybe I forgave him too easily. Maybe not. The way I see it, most people at least deserve second chances. I don't think what August and I had was something that could simply be thrown away over one stupid mistake he made, even if it felt like a pretty big one. I loved him, in some way, and I was willing to work on being able to trust him when he said he wouldn't leave me like that again.

Plus, he'd have to work for it. If he wanted to make up for the pain he had caused me, I was sure as hell gonna make sure he did it right.

SOLID EIGHT OUT OF TEN

THE DEEPLY BURIED, evil, sadistic part of myself did briefly consider making August get down on the sidewalk before me and beg for my forgiveness. Then I came to my senses. (Sadly.) Where's the fun in coming to your senses, am I right?

Anyway, I did forgive him. I forgave him and then I kissed him, because I'd been wanting to do that for DAYS. Don't even get me started. After you've had a taste of something so good, you might as well be having drug withdrawal when it's gone.

We sat on that bench and talked for a while. The sun was starting to go down by the time he pointed out that it was getting late. Ava was probably having a heart attack wondering where I was, because I answered none of the five missed phone calls or ten texts she sent me. Oops. No worries. She was going to forget all about that and be super happy for me once she found out where I had been.

Things were right in the world again. In fact, things were so right in the world that I left a glowing review on the Dating

Experiment's website, even considering the little hiccup. It had worked after all, in the long run, even for Ava. Obviously, I can't say that it worked out for everyone, as I don't have the statuses of all the pairs that participated, but it worked for me, August, Ava, and Klare, and so far Katie, so all of those other people didn't matter.

-

Days went by, and then weeks, and then months, and suddenly we were over a year past the first time we'd met. After several careful, well-monitored get-togethers, Luna and Cinnabun were doing just fine. Luna learned very quickly that Cinnabun just wasn't going to be the kind of playful sister she may have been hoping for. And August stayed.

In fact, all was so well in that department, as well as our relationship, that a few months short of our one year anniversary, August asked me to move in with him! (I know, right? You can squeal with joy. I already did.) Of course, that meant I also accepted his offer.

I know it may seem soon to some people, and maybe it was, but we had also revisited the idea of getting married and having children. Personally, August didn't want to get too much older before we started that, and I can't say I believed we needed to. Was it going to happen in that first year? Clearly not. The second year, though, well, options were open.

I figured, if he proposed sometime during our second year, then we'd get married about a year later and, hopefully, be expecting a child shortly after. I mean, I agreed, we didn't want to wait too long for practical reasons. And boyyyy was that baby going to be *cute*! (Obviously, I hoped s/he would have my red hair and his green eyes. Maybe my freckles too.) I hoped for a girl.

Yeah. I had this *all* planned out. Maybe that's a millennial thing. Like... we move fast. Couldn't tell ya.

Ava was both sad and happy, as was I. Once again, we were going our separate ways. Although, if I'm going to be perfectly honest, she couldn't have been too upset to see me go. After all, she found a new roommate in Klare pretty quickly after I had officially moved out. So, they were doing well also.

Katie was excited for me, obviously. We'd hung out more, and she introduced me to her other friends. We did things like go to movies, and shopping, and sipping wine in each other's living rooms as we gossiped. I loved it. I got out of the apartment so much more than I ever used to, even though I now definitely had a reason to want to stay in. (Queue suggestive winking.)

But in all seriousness, I really was genuinely happy and content with my life for the first time in a long time. I suppose I never realized how much I wasn't before, but sometimes that's just how life is. You can't always see what you're missing until it hits you right in the face. You don't realize you're even missing out on anything, because you're not out there looking for it in the first place.

I guess that only leaves me with one thing left to go over. My (legitimate) formal evaluation of the Dating Experiment, which I opted into even though I'd already been tricked into the *first* evaluation. Different circumstances now. I *had* to share my thoughts and feelings about the whole thing.

Question One: How would you rate your overall experience?

I guess a solid 8/10. There was the whole Reveal Ball thing I had to take into account.

Question Two: Would you recommend our services to a close friend or family member?

Definitely!

Question Three: Did you get out of this experience everything that you had been hoping for?

Surprisingly yes. Thoroughly shocked and still partially in disbelief, but still a yes.

Question Four: Is there any aspect of the Dating Experiment that you believe we could improve upon?

Hmm... Tough one. Probably not. I'd say you should always listen to your clients one hundred percent when they specify their preferences, but if you *had* done that, I wouldn't have this amazing, adorable, sweet, funny, and beautiful man that I find myself lucky to be with. So I guess... keep disregarding people's answers if you think you know better? It totally worked out in my/his case.

Any additional information you'd like to share with us?

Uh. Yeah. This whole thing sounded like the dumbest idea when my sister first proposed it to me. I mean, I literally just laughed, because I thought she was joking. I'd heard about the Dating Experiment before, but honest to God I thought it was either for Furries, (Just uh... Google that yourself,) or that it was for super desperate people who probably had no other choice.

And, yeah, I know what you're probably thinking. Ouch! Why would I shit on those people? Well, you're right. I shouldn't have been so judge-y about the whole thing, even if I'd been correct. That is a personal character flaw that I'll keep in mind for future reference. I promise.

The thing is, I learned that the Dating Experiment is so much more than that. It went way beyond my expectations, and therefore I would like to formally apologize for my previous misconceptions, even though, up until this very evaluation, you were, in fact, unaware of them. I suppose I could have just let that go and you never would have been the wiser. Oh well.

You guys rock. Keep doing what you're doing!

-Ella Carter

So there you have it. If you're single and ready to mingle, consider going a little (or a lot in my case) outside of your comfort zone. Try something new. Screw the traditional methods of finding someone. Experiment. (Maybe minus the animal heads) But trust me! You'll find love in places you never would have expected to find it if you keep an open mind.

The Dating Experiment

www.ingramcontent.com/pod-product-compliance
Lightning Source LLC
Chambersburg PA
CBHW071146170626
46809CB00002B/798